DOMINIQUE HAD TO LIE...

"Something worrying you?" he asked.

She avoided his eyes. "It's just that when I got here . . . to Antibes, I mean . . . I was with someone . . . And we had a row. . . ."

He put his hands over his ears. "I don't want to hear! It's none of my business. You're landed up here now, and that's all that matters, as far as I'm concerned."

"But it isn't! You must listen!" She was close to tears.

He lowered his hands. "All right, fire away!"

"He was awful to me! I never want to see him again! But he'll be looking for me all over the place. He may come down here, to the harbor. And if he finds me . . ."

"I get it."

"So you musn't let anyone know I'm here! No one!"

WOMAN HUNT

FRANCIS RYCK

A FAWCETT CREST BOOK

Fawcett Publications, Inc., Greenwich, Connecticut

WOMAN HUNT

THIS BOOK CONTAINS THE COMPLETE TEXT
OF THE ORIGINAL HARDCOVER EDITION.

A Fawcett Crest Book reprinted by arrangement
with Stein and Day, Inc.

Library of Congress Catalog Card Number: 72-755510

Printed in the United States of America
August 1973

WOMAN HUNT

ONE

After zipping up his mechanic's overalls, he took a camera from his tool kit and slipped it into one of his pockets. Then he stuffed the flashlight and the nylon rope, wound around the grappling hook, into his haversack. As always, his movements were precise and self-assured.

Sylvia tried to remember the words to the melody that he was whistling softly through his teeth as he headed toward the bathroom. She heard the tap run and could picture him bending over the sink, drinking from his cupped hands. Curling up, she pulled the bedclothes more snugly around her.

She had such confidence in him now that she no longer felt any twinges of anxiety: she *knew* that everything would go according to his carefully worked-out plans and that he would come back safely.

During the three months that she had been his mistress, she had learned nothing of his past and very little of his present. He was a man of extraordinary reticence. From the very beginning, she had been willing to accept the long, unexplained absences and the unannounced returns, which seldom lasted for more than two or three days: she had not even resented his habit of turning away her questions with a good-natured, enigmatic smile. When, at last, he had confided in her what his job really was, she had felt immensely exhilarated, as though he had bestowed on her some kind of accolade.

As he came back from the bathroom, she looked fondly at his calm, reliable face, with its prominent cheekbones and green eyes beneath a thatch of thick dark hair. He approached the bed and laid a firm hand on her shoulder. Sliding down, she pressed her cheek against it, smiling, with her eyes closed.

His job, as he had explained it to her, required imagination and daring, and he was admirably suited to it. Though not strictly legal, it did not involve him in anything nasty like trafficking in drugs or in common or garden housebreaking.

What he did was to get hold of secret manufacturing processes of one kind or another and sell them to competitors. In a way, it was sort of a game . . .

Kola sat down on the bed and kissed her. She flung an arm around his neck, hugging him to her.

"We're partners now, aren't we . . . as well as everything else?" she said softly.

Kola smiled, with his eyes on the alarm clock on the bedside table. It was just after midnight.

"You must admit, you couldn't have done without me this time," she persisted.

He sat up and asked her, patiently, where she had put the plan. Patience was an essential quality in his profession.

"In the wardrobe drawer. You know it is." She was looking at him with an expression of amused indulgence, which always irritated him.

He got off the bed, took the three sheets of paper from the drawer, and put them in his pocket.

"You can't still need them! You've learned them by heart!"

"Can't be too careful." He smiled down at her. "Now be a good girl, and go to sleep."

"I'll try."

"There's nothing to worry about. I'll have finished by three. Leaves me plenty of time to catch the four o'clock to Paris, and I'll be back tomorrow evening with the money." He was merely repeating what he had told her several times before in the same calm, reassuring voice, as though talking to a child.

Sylvia waved him good-by with a sickeningly coy wiggle of her fingers, then ran a hand through the darkening roots of her dyed blond hair. She was anxious for him to stop looking at her and leave, uncomfortably aware that her face was wrinkled and swollen under the harsh electric light. It was only when they made love in the dark that she could still feel like a girl of sixteen.

Kola took a last sharp glance around the room, as he always did before leaving. Sylvia put it down to sentiment; a desire to implant every detail of their love nest in his mind. He slipped the straps of his haversack over his shoulders and picked up his tool kit. He never left any of his personal belongings behind when he went on one of his expeditions.

"Couldn't you leave your things here just till to-morrow evening?" Sylvia teased.

"I like to have them with me. I might want them . . ."

She burst out laughing. "With those overalls of yours and your tool kit, you look as if you were really going to work in the factory!"

He stared at her blankly: she found that he rarely enjoyed her sense of humor. Clearing his throat, he said insistently, "Now, remember. Act perfectly normally when you get to the office tomorrow.

They won't know anyone's been there, so there's no reason to be nervous."

"Of course I will, darling." She screwed up her eyes. "All I'll be thinking of is our cottage in the country. We'll be able to buy it when you come back with all that lovely money."

She really was ugly as sin. Kola raised a hand in farewell, as though he was seeing her off at a railway station.

He did not take the elevator, but walked down the fifteen floors, past the long, dimly lit corridors. The apartment building was as vast as a prison and gave out the same muffled sounds. His bicycle, with the small auxiliary engine, was parked in the courtyard: he strapped his tool kit to its carrier and wheeled it out into the road. The wide avenue, running between the Villeurbanne skyscrapers, was deserted.

He got on and pedaled till the engine started. There was an eight-mile journey ahead of him. The whole Lyon suburb seemed fast asleep, hibernating, and even when he reached the Décines road, he met no traffic beyond an occasional truck. Despite the sheepskin vest beneath his overalls, the cold stabbed through him, increasing his impatience to get on with the job.

As soon as the factory came into sight, he concealed his bicycle in the ditch and covered the last five hundred yards on foot. With its twinkling lights, the factory stood out like some strange, rectilinear monument, composed of cubular buildings, concrete tanks, soaring chimneys, elevated pipes, and metal catwalks. The night shift was on, but it seemed to have a pulsating life of its own, unconnected with them.

Kola moved off the road and walked along the grass shoulder. He had reconnoitered the terrain, once by daylight and once by night, at the same time as now. Passing the main gates and the watchman's box, he kept on at a steady pace, hugging the wall. The factory's monotonous hum was increasing in volume, and he could smell faint whiffs of ammonia fumes.

Its lights lit up the frozen grass outside for a distance of four hundred yards; beyond came a stretch of darkness, where the wall forked. This was the site of the administration buildings, approached by another road, with a separate entrance. Protected by night patrols and an automatic alarm system, it was a highly dangerous area in which to operate. He could safely gain access to it only from above, starting from the workshop sector on his left and then following the route that Sylvia had mapped out for him.

He stopped twenty yards short of the dark zone and swept his flashlight rapidly over the ground until he located the stone that he had placed against the wall during his daylight recon. It marked a spot arrowed by Sylvia on the photo-

graph she had taken a week before. Unwinding
the nylon rope, he tossed up the grappling hook,
which caught fast on the top of the wall at his first
attempt. He climbed up, detached the hook, and
wound the rope around his waist. Then he jumped
down onto the concrete roof of a small shed just
below him. From now on, he would have to follow
Sylvia's directions blindly.

He moved cautiously across the shed till his
hands came in contact with curved, metal rungs
set into the wall of a building, rising sixty feet
above him; then he began to climb. The frozen
steel burned into his fingers, and the pain had become acute by the time he hauled himself up onto
the flat roof. It was bathed in a pale light, reflected from some source that he could not place. Pre-
ceded by the white vapor of his breath, he crossed
to the far side, noting the memorized landmarks
on the way, unwound the rope again, and fixed the
hook to the parapet. If Sylvia was right, he had to
lower himself fifteen feet onto another flat roof,
but this could only be an approximate guess; with
the side of the building in complete darkness, it
was impossible for him to make his own assess-
ment.

He slid slowly down the rope with his arms at
full stretch but reached the end of it with his feet
still dangling in the air. He peered down between
his legs, hoping to glimpse the roof, but he might
as well have been looking down a well. There was

13

nothing he could do but let go. He did, and hit the
concrete a mere four inches below. Even so, it had
been an unnerving experience. Standing on tiptoe,
not daring to step backward, he jerked at the rope
to release the hook. It seemed to have become embedded, and a good five minutes passed before he
managed to dislodge it.

His route now resembled an assault course laid
out by a sadistic drill sergeant. He leaped across a
five-foot gap between two buildings onto a sloping
roof, climbed up a skylight vibrating from machin-
ery in the workshop underneath, pulled himself
across a section of elevated pipe, and edged his
way along a thirty-foot ledge, scarcely wide
enough to take his feet, with a sheer drop of sixty
feet below him.

More metal rungs brought him to yet another
roof, where he fixed his grappling hook in align-
ment with two of the factory's chimneys, then slid
down the rope till his feet came to rest on a win-
dowsill. The window was ajar, and a push opened
it wide enough for him to scramble through into
the office. Sylvia had carried out her part of the
job with admirable efficiency.

He shut the window behind him and crouched
down in the darkness for a moment or two, absolutely still. Though he was sweating all over, his
fingers remained numb, and he had to blow on
them to restore their circulation. Then he stood
up, drew the curtains, and switched on his flash-

light. The office, smelling of stale cigarette smoke, was strictly functional, though comfortable enough, with a thick gray carpet, a revolving chair behind a walnut desk, and two large leather armchairs in front of it. A single metal filing cabinet took up most of one wall; the built-in safe stood facing it.

Putting his flashlight down on the desk, he rubbed his hands together and flexed his fingers, like a pianist before a performance. It was one of his small vanities. The key of the safe was in the third drawer of the desk from the bottom, as Sylvia had told him it would be, and, to his relief, the combination she had given him—5-4-22—had undergone no last-minute change. He swung the door open, pausing to memorize the exact order and position of the files before taking them out one by one.

The file for which he was looking was enclosed in a green cardboard folder, with no heading or reference number to indicate its contents. Once he had found it, he closed the safe again and kneeling under the desk, flashlight between his teeth, began to photograph its pages, separating them with his fingernail. There were eighty-seven in all, devoted to the various manufacturing processes of an abrasive liquid, recently discovered by research chemists in LICOM's laboratories. In the fields of optics and metallurgy, it represented a major breakthrough. But better informed than Sylvia, the organization for which Kola worked was aware that the Ministry of Defense had a priority claim on the new discovery, that the formulas that he was photographing were destined to play a far greater role than merely placing LICOM ahead of its industrial rivals.

After a momentary interruption while he reloaded his camera, he took the final shots and replaced the file in its former position. Then, putting on a pair of gloves, he wiped his fingerprints off the safe, desk, and window, and left.

The return journey taxed him even more than the first one, demanding acrobatic feats that all his experience in mountain climbing had scarcely prepared him for. By the end of it, every muscle was aching agonizingly. It had taken him seventeen minutes to reach the office, but he needed a good half hour to reach the far side of the wall again. Behind his satisfaction at having brought off the mission, there was a slight feeling of resentment that he should have been on his own, a one-man band, throughout the operation. But at least, on this occasion, the stakes had been worthwhile . . .

TWO

Kola rang up Sylvia from a telephone booth in the station at Les Brotteaux. It was a long time before she answered, and he wondered, irritably, how anyone could sleep as soundly as that. He could picture her in the warm bed, lying with her cheek on the palm of her hand, making the little nibbling movements with her lips, as though she were actually tasting her sleep. When she finally lifted the receiver, she announced, "Sylvia Barsouin," in her office voice.

"It's me," Kola said. "Everything's fine, but I want you to do something for me."

He was prepared to wait patiently now till she emerged from her torpor. It always took her ages to wake up. Bleary-eyed, her face smothered in night cream, she would be struggling to raise herself onto her elbows.

Eventually she asked, "Where are you?"

He smiled into the mouthpiece and adopted his gentle tone of voice. "Sure you're really awake? That's my girl! I'm just catching the train, and I want you to pick up a package that I've left on the Quai du Rhône—the far side, opposite the exhibition buildings. You take the steps on your right when you've crossed the footbridge and then turn right again at the bottom. You'll see a pile of sand straight in front of you. Opposite it, there's a small hole in the wall, must have been a pipe there at some time. That's where I've left the package. Keep it in the apartment till I get back tomorrow."

"Is it the ... ?"

"No, just something of mine I don't want to have on me, after all. You'll understand when you see it. And, by the way, don't take your car. It's safer if you come on foot."

"Why? What can happen?"

"Nothing. But it always pays to be careful." He heard a snicker of laughter and closed his eyes, then added, "Hurry, darling! Please!"

Now there was the sound of a juicy kiss, and he had to force himself to send one back.

"I hope you haven't caught cold?" Sylvia asked.

"I'm too frozen at the moment to know. See you tomorrow!" He hung up, grateful to her for not making difficulties. There were not many women who would have agreed to come out at this hour of the morning without grumbling.

He got back on his bicycle and headed toward the spot to which he just directed her. It seemed to be getting still colder, and he ran into a thin drizzle as he approached the river. The sidewalks were deserted, and only a few cars swished by on the road, with a yellowish halo around their headlights. Farther on, he met a couple of policemen, pedaling lethargically around their beat; their capes fluttered gently like fins, making them resemble large fish idling around some subterranean grotto.

The Rhône swirled past, heavy from the rains of the previous week and lemon-colored beneath the lights on the bridge. Once he had crossed it, he hoisted his bicycle onto his shoulder and went down the steps. After a glance around to make certain there was no one to see him, he walked back under the bridge, unstrapped his tool kit, and slid the bike into the river.

Moving back to the wall, he slipped his hand into the hiding place he had described to Sylvia and drew out the package, which he had deposited there five days before on his arrival in Lyon. He unwrapped it and palmed the two small objects it contained. There was nothing to do now but wait. The time was 3:20.

Exhausted, he leaned back against the wall, where the bridge threw its deepest shadow. He would have given anything for a cigarette and a scalding cup of tea, followed by twelve hours' uninterrupted sleep. The damp cold rose all around him, mingling with the smell from the river and the dull thuds of branches swept against the stonework.

Twenty minutes later, he heard the sharp tap of Sylvia's footsteps coming down to the quay. Only thirty-five minutes had elapsed since his telephone call: she had come extraordinarily quickly. Allowing for the time that it must have taken her to get dressed—and she would certainly have exchanged her night cream for day cream before leaving the apartment—it was clear that she must have cheated, come part of the way, at least, by taxi. But he bore her no ill will for cutting down his wait.

In another minute, he could see her approaching, wobbling along on her high heels. She was peering in front of her, with her neck stretched out like a hen's. When she reached the pile of sand, she did a right turn to the wall and began groping up and down it; fruitlessly, since the hiding place, in fact, was three yards farther on.

He broke the vial into the absorbent cotton and

came up behind her in three quick silent strides. Clapping the pad over her nose and mouth with one hand, he gripped the back of her neck with the other. She scarcely struggled—merely jerked her shoulders two or three times, as though trying to get rid of a knapsack. Then her legs gave way under her, and she slipped to the ground. He slid down with her, keeping the chloroform-soaked pad tight against her face. The longer it stayed there, the better; he did not want her to suffer unnecessarily. She would not have seen anything or realized what was happening, and that was as it should be.

He looked up and down the quay again before dragging her under the bridge and dropping her into the river, as he had done with his bicycle. Her body sank immediately, carried down slantwise by the current. In this weather, it would not come to the surface for at least a week after becoming caught in the sluices at the Guillotière. There would be no signs of violence. Her death would be put down to suicide or accident. It did not matter which.

He set out briskly for the station at Perrache, to all appearances a tired night-shift worker in a hurry to get home, which, basically, was not far from the truth. Now that Sylvia had been disposed of, he could think of her with gratitude that almost amounted to affection. All the exasperation that he

21

had had to disguise whenever they had been together had evaporated with her body's disappearance into the eddies of the Rhône.

It was a relief to have it over and done with, for he had often longed to kill her when compelled to look at her and listen to her endless chattering, a revolting mishmash of sentimentality and stale jokes. Each time he had come back to her, he had inwardly recoiled at the sight of her, her coy glances, the abominable way she dressed, and her preoccupation with any new makeup advertised in women's magazines. Above all, he detested her insistence on making what she called love according to certain recipes of her own, as if it were *poule-au-riz* or *boeuf miroton*. In the end he had come to hate her, just as he hated everything in her apartment, an avant-garde monstrosity with mobiles hanging from the ceiling, hideous curtains, and a bookcase filled with hair-raising erotica. The way she pulled on her stockings was enough, in itself, to turn his thoughts to murder.

Still, as she had pointed out, he could not have done without her. And if her reward had not been quite what she expected . . . well, everyone had his disappointments. Or nearly everyone . . .

These reflections occupied him till he came to the Place de Terreaux, empty except for four benumbed and disgruntled pigeons, squatting by the fountain. Remembering his last careful glance around the apartment before leaving it a few hours before, he felt confident that he had left nothing behind to betray his temporary residence there. If Sylvia had mentioned him to her colleagues at the office, it would have been as Nicolas Balsier, insurance agent. There was no reason for anyone to relate this identity to his other one. Nor was there any danger from the other tenants in the building. It was so enormous that they paid as little attention to each other as to fellow passengers on the subway. And, lastly, there was no chance of his final telephone call being traced. He had covered all his tracks.

By the time he reached the Place Bellecour, he had dismissed the whole matter from his mind, as though it were a past illness, on which it would be profitless to dwell. The town was slowly coming awake, as early-morning workers emerged into the drizzle. At Perrache a few passengers, bundled up and sleepy-eyed, were lugging their suitcases down the station steps.

He went through the usual routine to make certain that he was not being followed before buying a ticket to Paris, then collected a large leather suitcase from the automatic lockers and bolted himself into a restroom cubicle, where he exchanged his overalls and sheepskin vest for a tweed overcoat from the bag. After slipping the two rolls of microfilm into his trouser pocket, he stuffed everything else, clothes, haversack, and tool kit, into the bag and, with a quarter of an hour to spare before his train came in, shaved himself with his battery-operated razor. Somehow, this helped him to shed a little of his fatigue.

He drank a cup of coffee, bitter but hot, on the platform and lit the cigarette that he had been keeping for this first moment of relaxation. A bath would have been extremely welcome, but it would have to wait. One small pleasure at a time . . .

He gulped down a second cup of coffee to insure his keeping awake during the journey. With what he had on him, sleep was out of the question. Though everything pointed to his being completely safe, he was far too much of a professional to trust to appearances.

When the train came in, he waited till the very last minute to jump into a second-class car at the front, then walked through to the back and settled down in an empty first-class compartment. Stretched out, apparently asleep, he kept a sharp eye open for the comings and goings in the corridor outside.

After half an hour, his subconscious took over. From long experience, he knew that it would allow nothing to escape it, that it was a thoroughly reliable piece of mechanism. He employed it even when on vacation and would continue to do so after he had given up his present profession. Endowed with perpetual motion, it had become second nature to him. Thanks to its assistance, he had reached the age of forty-six, and he hoped to live a great deal longer.

The train got in to Paris just after midday. The weather was as cold as it had been in Lyon, though less humid, and the town had a gray, frosty look. Kola mixed with the crowds going down to the Métro, milled around with them for half a minute, and then came back up again into the concourse of the main station. He called Françoise from a pay phone.

There was no answer. If she had gone out, something must be wrong because her orders were to stay in and wait for his call over the last three days. He waited a couple of minutes and dialed the number again in case she had been in the bathroom. There was still no answer, and a third attempt was equally fruitless. He felt vaguely uneasy but not particularly surprised. Everything had gone much too smoothly up till now.

He always expected snags to crop up sooner or later and came near to resenting the suspense when they were late in appearing. Consequently, it was almost with relief that he confronted the present one. His main source of worry was his own exhaustion, which left him in a state of feverish drowsiness, like that preceding an illness.

Contacts did not make mistakes or go out on their own business when they were supposed to stay in. Above all, Françoise, with whom he had worked for a long time. So a telephone ringing in an empty room was tantamount to an alarm signal. After a moment's reflection, he called the dance studio where she often went to practice. It was only as he finished dialing that it occurred to him that everyone would probably be out to lunch, but a feminine voice answered promptly, told him that Françoise was there, and sent someone to fetch her.

"I was waiting for you to call," Françoise said placidly. "Pierre was sure you'd think of calling here."

Pierre was head of the network.

"Not ill, is he?" Kola asked.

"Just a touch of flu. We're all a bit under the weather at the moment, but it's nothing serious. I dropped you a line, as a matter of fact, to let you know. How are things with you?"

"Fine! I've been pretty busy, but I'll be able to take it easier now. See you soon!" He hung up.

In plain language, this meant that the network had run into some kind of trouble in Paris and that there would be a message waiting for him, general delivery, in the Rue de Rennes.

Now that he had been warned, it was vital to avoid any kind of risk. He stuffed the two rolls of microfilm into the bottom of his bag and deposited it at the baggage checkroom, then mailed the receipt to himself, general delivery, the central post office. It would get there by the following morning. Having taken this precaution, he could face whatever difficulties had occurred with equanimity.

He took a taxi to the Rue de Rennes and picked up Françoise's letter. Typed, it had been composed with her customary terseness: *"Three hours after your telephone call. Tobacconist in the Place Saint-Georges. Francoise."*

The signature, handwritten as usual, with the cedilla missing from under the "c," was undoubtedly hers. He had telephoned her just after 12:30, which meant that their rendezvous was at 3:30. More with the idea of building up his strength than from hunger, he took another taxi to the Coupole and lunched on a dozen oysters and a thick, rare steak. He drank nothing with the meal but ordered two cups of coffee after it, relaxed and unconcerned for the moment with what lay ahead. There would be plenty of time to worry about that in an hour or two, when his meeting with Françoise approached. Whatever threat had put the network in a state of alert, he would inevitably become involved in it if he kept the appointment; but there was no way of avoiding it. It was just one more risk on top of all the others.

The worst part of the whole business was that security precautions prevented him even from telephoning Dominique, who had been expecting him back the day before. As far as she was concerned, he was a dealer in antiques, who made trips from time to time to replenish the stock of his shop in the Rue Bonaparte. She could have no inkling that there was any other side to his life than the one he presented to her.

At 2:55 he paid his bill, took a cab from the taxi stand opposite the restaurant, and told the driver to take him to La Muette. He had yielded to a sudden impulse, an absurd piece of sentimentality wholly foreign to him, without pausing to consider whether Dominique would be in at this hour of the day. In the circumstances, it scarcely mattered whether she was or not. At La Muette, he instructed the driver to go slowly down the Avenue Mozart; then, leaning forward, he stared up as they passed the apartment. The sight of the windows on the third floor was enough to give him a momentary illusion of hearing her light footsteps coming toward him, of seeing her toss her scarf onto the back of a chair, of being back up there with her. The little confined world, which meant everything to him, was only a few yards away, but, he reflected sourly, for all practical purposes it might as well have been in the Antipodes.

Slumping back in his seat, he was embarrassed to find the driver eyeing him impassively in the rear-view mirror and told him sharply to drop him in the Place Saint-Georges. He was angry with himself for his moment of weakness. He could only attribute it to nervous exhaustion.

He stopped the cab before it reached the square and covered the last hundred yards on foot. It was 3:15, and the same gray light still persisted. People were hurrying along in the bitter cold, red-nosed, and huddled up inside their overcoats. As he passed the tobacconist's, he glanced inside. There were a few men standing up at the counter and a couple of women seated at a table, with steaming cups in front of them. Françoise had not yet arrived.

Memorizing the telephone number printed in gold on the shop window, he headed toward Trinité Church. When he came to a bar, he went inside and waited till 3:40 before telephoning the tobacconist's and asking for Mademoiselle Oscarsen. He could hear the proprietor calling out the name and in a matter of seconds Françoise was on the line. He told her to meet him inside Trinité, and she agreed without comment. She would be expecting him to take additional precautions.

He entered the square from the side opposite the church. Two small children, blue with cold, were chasing each other unenthusiastically, watched over by a stoical English nurse, sitting stiffly on a bench, with her hands tucked into her sleeves, like a nun. In ten minutes he saw Françoise approaching with long, athletic strides.

She was wearing slacks, and her black hair was
tied in a ponytail. Hands deep in the pockets of a
light trench coat, she looked as comfortable and
relaxed as if it had been a fine spring day. He
watched her skirt the square and walk up the
steps into the church. There was no sign of anyone
tailing her, but to be on the safe side, he waited
another few minutes before following her in.

She was sitting behind a column, out of sight of
two old women telling their beads at the far end of
the nave. He touched her lightly on the shoulder
as he passed and went out by a side door. She
joined him a moment later, smiling, as if it were all
a game.

"You look like a spy who forgot to come in out of
the cold," she said, and slipped her arm through
his as they walked down the steps.

She was as tall as he was, with a slight, singsong
Swedish accent, which squared with the surname
of Oscarsen; her Christian name, she had once told
him, came from a French mother. Beyond this, he
knew nothing of her background or of what had
induced her to join the network. It was none of his
concern, and he had never felt any desire to probe
into it.

"I'm not at the old address," she informed him.
"Pierre heard that the police had been around
talking to his concierge, and Stani got it into his
head that he was shadowed when he went to Marseille, so you can imagine what's been going on.

Tight security, everyone lying low, all the usual stuff. And as I gather you're particularly hot, I was told to move."

Kola nodded, relieved. Things were not as bad as he had feared. It sounded as though this were another of the alarms that occurred from time to time, triggered off by routine inquiries quite unconnected with the network's activities. But they had to be taken seriously until it could be established that everyone was in the clear.

"I'm in the Rue Clauzel now," Françoise added.

She would be in one of the apartments, bought or rented by the network in France and elsewhere, to serve as hideouts for its members when the necessity arose. These apartments were disposed of and others substituted for them quite legally through real estate agents every few months, and provided cover with a high degree of security.

"Is Pierre there?" Kola asked.

"No. He wants you to stay with me till he turns up." She grinned at him. "It's minute, and there's only one bed, but as you look all in, I'll sacrifice myself and sleep on the floor. You can't say that isn't a fair offer!"

He did not respond to her lightheartedness. "You mean, he won't be coming today?"

"No. He might tomorrow, maybe later. I'm afraid you'll just have to wait."

They had begun walking back up the street, jostled by the crowds on the narrow pavement. "Just have to wait . . ." Kola felt a surge of anger but knew that it would serve no purpose to give vent to it. He would obey orders because it would be unthinkable to do otherwise. "Tomorrow, maybe later . . ." Pierre and those above him who directed the network as if it were an impersonal machine were playing hell with his private life. To them, of course, it was no more than a convenient cover for his other activities.

Separated from him by a thrusting pedestrian, Françoise fought her way back and took his arm again. He was too much absorbed by his personal problems to notice a woman approaching on the opposite sidewalk, whose glance rested on him for a moment before passing on to Françoise. The woman slowed down and seemed to hesitate, as though she could not believe what she had seen, then crossed the road and fell in behind them, with a dozen or so pedestrians in between.

She was in her early thirties, wearing a sealskin coat and high thigh boots. Her masculine appearance was accentuated by closely cut hair, a leather bag slung over one shoulder, and a cigarette stuck in the corner of her mouth. Presently, she let the cigarette fall to the pavement without taking her eyes off the couple ahead. She was now only a few yards behind them.

The apartment, on the fourth floor of an unpretentious building, consisted of a living room, a bedroom, a kitchen scarcely larger than a cupboard, and a bathroom. Kola noticed appreciatively that the low, wide bed looked comfortable and that the central heating was working. Françoise's presence over the last few days was betrayed by little more than the unmade bed, four suitcases piled up in a corner of the bedroom, and a record player and a pile of records lying on the green carpet. There were no personal belongings in the way of books or photographs. She had installed herself, as in the last two apartments that Kola had visited, as though she were a one-night guest in a hotel.

He slumped down on the bed without taking off his overcoat. Françoise removed hers and hung it in a closet.

"You look absolutely dead beat," she remarked. "Do you want something to eat? Or a drink?"

"Sleep's all I want. Unless you happen to have some aspirin or antiflu stuff?"

She burst out laughing. With her high-necked sweater and ponytail, she looked like a first-year student.

"Oh, no! Don't tell me you've *really* got flu! Now I'll catch it and give it to everyone else. Must be the power of suggestion. I shouldn't have mentioned it on the phone." She went into the bathroom and came back with a bottle. "Here's some aspirin! I'd better make you a hot toddy to go with it. Luckily, I've got some whiskey." As she went out again, she added over her shoulder, "If there's anything you want to hide, do it while I'm in the kitchen."

Kola began to undress. The films were safe enough where they were, and, in any case, he could not get hold of them till the following morning. He would have given a lot to soak in a hot bath, but when he glanced into the bathroom, he found that it contained only a shower. As he unbuttoned his shirt, he automatically looked out of the window. There was nothing in the street to attract his attention, but this did not mean a thing, as he very well knew. If anyone was watching the apartment, he would scarcely have stationed himself in full view on the opposite sidewalk.

He threw his shirt onto an armchair as Françoise came back with a steaming mug. She stood contemplating his chest in half-mocking admiration.

"Quite a muscleman, aren't you? Nice tan, too. How do you manage it? Push-ups and a sun lamp?"

He smiled without answering her and began sipping the toddy. In the last few months he had become a trifle sensitive about his age. Françoise drew the curtains and lit the bedside lamp. The bedroom suddenly became intimate and cozy.

"I'll just straighten out the bed," she said.

"No, leave it as it is." Kola yawned. "I'm only sorry it isn't still warm."

"We can share it tonight, if you like."

Kola shrugged and got in. "It'd certainly be more comfortable."

She bent down and felt his forehead. "You've got a fever, all right. How about some more whiskey?"

"Sleep . . . first . . ." Kola muttered, and immediately dropped off.

THREE

Dominique replaced the receiver. She had just telephoned the shop for the fourth time, and, for the fourth time, Percy had told her in his affected voice that he had not heard from Monsieur Nicolas. She was in a state of frustration and anxiety bordering on hysteria. Kola had never been late before in returning from one of his buying trips. Now he was three days overdue, and she had no means of communicating with him. Despite her protests, he always refused to leave her an address —whether he went to the provinces or abroad— under the pretext that he was continually on the move and never knew from one night to the next where he would be staying. When she had broached the subject again before his present trip to Italy, he had turned on her with unexpected sharpness.

She glanced at her watch. Three o'clock. Crossing to the window, she peered down into the street. She had made the same short journey innumerable times during the last three days and, the night before, had jumped out of bed to look out each time she had thought she heard a car draw up in front of the apartment building. The wind had changed, bringing rain from the west, which beat against the glass and added to her depression.

She turned away abruptly, took a bottle of brandy from an antique wine cooler, and carried it into the bedroom. Pouring herself a stiff drink, she gulped it down with her eyes closed. The taste of alcohol disgusted her, and normally she never touched it, but she had begun to take regular nips to anesthetize herself against the intolerable waiting.

She had taken a bath that morning, but had not had the energy to do her hair or get dressed; she had merely slipped into the heavy Chinese dressing gown that Kola had given her as a wedding present three years before and gone back to bed, locking herself in until the cleaning woman left.

Kola's instinctive good taste had been responsible for the decoration and furnishing of the whole apartment, which he had filled with the best pieces picked up on his expeditions. She sometimes felt that she was living in an annex of the antique shop and that she herself was just another precious item in the collection, that perhaps he had only married her because he had realized that there was no other way of acquiring her.

Her bedroom was "period," down to the brushes and perfume bottles on her dressing table. Kola had said that he had designed the room around her, and it was true that there was something about her, evocative of old-fashioned miniatures, that somehow was "period" too. Something in the slenderness of her neck, her chestnut curls, her periwinkle-blue eyes, and what he called her marquise look. She had an unstudied aloofness, an air of looking down at life from a theater box, which had alternately amused and infuriated her fellow students during her year at the Beaux-Arts.

The contempt she had always felt for jealous wives had not stopped her from searching Kola's pockets and papers in his desk for some evidence of an affair. When she had failed to find any, she had been ashamed of the impulse, though she could have pleaded some justification for it. In the last few months he had been noticeably irritable and withdrawn, as though some new element had come into his life that he could not confide to her. And he had become far more preoccupied with physical fitness than he had been at the beginning of their marriage. She had found herself living with a stranger, in a sense deeper than the mere fact that she was French and Nicolas Krestowicz was Polish.

Nevertheless, she could not believe that Kola's absence was due to another woman, that the affection and need for her that he had continued to display despite the change in his personality had been anything but genuine. And even if she accepted that he was capable of indulging in some casual love affair, he would certainly have covered up, telephoned her with some plausible explanation for his delay. An accident appeared to be the only solution; yet this, too, was open to objection. He must have his passport, visiting cards, and other means of identification on him. She would have been notified. Or if not she, Percy at the shop.

She had not left the apartment during the whole three days, afraid to miss a telephone call or a telegram, but she could not go on like this. She had scarcely eaten and was in danger of becoming a drunken wreck. She must get out, see someone, and be forced to regain some measure of self-control. A visit to Laura might do the trick. Laura's cynical outlook did not invite confidences or encourage self-pity.

After taking a cold shower and rubbing herself

down fiercely with a sponge, she put on a pair of slacks, boots, and a roomy sweater, which dated from her days at the Beaux-Arts, then dialed Laura's number.

"Hello, darling, I was wondering what had happened to you?" Laura said in the affectionate purr she always adopted toward her.

"Then why didn't you call me?" Dominique retorted. "Can I come over, or are you going out?"

"Is Kola back?"

"Not yet." Dominique meant to stop there, but her sense of grievance was too much for her. "He should have been back three days ago, and I haven't heard a word from him!"

There was a pause before Laura asked dryly, "I suppose you're in a hell of a state?"

"Well, naturally, I'm worried."

"In case he's had some ghastly accident? Put it out of your head, dear. He hasn't."

"How on earth can you know?"

"Experience. It's always a mistake to worry about husbands."

"All the same, he may . . ."

"Don't you believe it! Anyway, come on over. André's gone to Berlin for a couple of days, so we'll dine together, just the two of us, at that Russian place. And you can stay the night if you want to. I might even give you my best lavender sheets . . ."

The living room in Laura's apartment behind

the Avenue Foch had been decorated while she was going through a Scandinavian phase: it had ultramodern Swedish furniture, Danish wallpaper, and a wide brick fireplace. She herself, barefoot, in plum-colored trousers and tunic, was bending over the fire replacing a fallen log, a cigarette in her mouth and a whiskey and soda in her free hand.

"You just have to take these things in stride, sweetie," she said.

"Can't we talk about something else?" Dominique asked wearily.

"You'd still go on brooding, so what's the point?"

Laura screwed up her eyes and peered down at her in a way that made her feel acutely uncomfortable. It was somehow a man's look. Laura's masculinity, reflected in the gestures with which she had helped her off with her raincoat, poured her a drink, and lit her cigarette, had been rather agreeable—as if she were with a boyfriend—but this intrusive appraisal was quite another matter.

"It's tough, what you're going through," Laura went on, "but you'll get over it, you'll see."

Dominique managed a smile, though she was feeling dizzy. Whiskey on top of brandy had been a mistake, but Laura had insisted. All she wanted was to telephone home on the faint chance that Kola was back, but she was certain that Laura would despise her if she suggested it. Perhaps in a minute or two, as second best, she would be able to cook up an excuse for calling the office. In the meantime she said jauntily, "You seem to be making much more of a thing of this than I am. I've been sleeping badly lately and my nerves are a bit on edge, but I haven't gone nuts. I know perfectly well that Kola will be back in a day or two."

"Let's hope so," Laura said flatly. "But you can't fool me, pet. You're all on edge, and I don't blame you. So was I."

"So were you *when?*"

"When it happened to me, about a year after we were married. And I wasn't as lucky as you. I didn't have anyone to advise me."

Dominique frowned. "Honestly, I don't know what you're talking about!"

Laura sat down, leaning forward with her elbows on her knees. "Come off it, darling! You don't have to put on an act with me. You know damn well what I'm talking about. But if you want to stick your head in the sand and pretend everything's okay, that's fine. Just say so, and I'll shut up. On the other hand, if you want to be . . . well, realistic . . . maybe I can help."

Dominique glared at her. "I know damn well what you're hinting at, but you haven't a thing to go on."

"Unfortunately I have."

Dominique stubbed out her cigarette and took some time to light another one. "All right! Let's have it!"

"If you really want me to . . . You'll probably hate me. Still, I'm a good enough friend . . ."

"Oh, for God's sake! If you know where Kola is, tell me!"

"Well, he isn't in Italy, as you seem to think. He's here, in Paris."

"How do *you* know?"

"I saw him."

"When?"

"Day before yesterday. Near Trinité. He was on the other side of the road."

"By himself? . . . No, obviously not, or you wouldn't be making such a fuss. Who was he with? Anyone you know?"

"A young girl. She looked rather shabby. Never saw her before."

"Pretty?"

"Up to a point . . ."

Dominique said slowly, "So what? She could have been anyone. I mean . . ."

"Of course, darling. A client, or anyone . . . Only they *were* walking arm in arm."

"Maybe it wasn't Kola at all. Just someone who looked like him."

"It was Kola all right. I'd know that coat of his a mile off. Besides, I followed them."

"Followed them where?"

Laura looked at her, surprised. "You're taking it terribly well, darling. I was afraid you'd collapse. I suppose it was her place. An apartment in the Rue Clauzel."

Dominique got up. "Why on earth didn't you call me up at once and tell me?"

"It wasn't any of my business. I wouldn't have told you now if you hadn't asked me." Laura got up, too, and stretched out to take her hands.

Dominique ignored the gesture. "What's her name?"

"No idea. They went up to the fourth floor. That's all I know."

"You followed them as far as that?" Dominique's voice was contemptuous. "What ever for?"

On the defensive, Laura snapped back, "Really, what does it matter? I suppose because when I start something, I like to see it through."

"Then see it through by telling me the number!"

"Thirty-seven. But you . . ."

Dominique snatched up her raincoat from the sofa and headed for the front door. Laura followed, babbling, making ineffectual attempts to stop her. She was completely at a loss now that she was no longer the dominating one of the two. "Don't rush off like that! . . . Darling, you aren't going to . . . Well, perhaps you're right . . . But come straight back here!"

Without looking around, Dominique ran down the staircase, leaving the door of the apartment wide open behind her.

FOUR

||||||||||||||||||||||||||||||||||||||||||||||||||||||||||||||||||||||||||||||||||||||||||||

Pierre had not yet put in an appearance.

Françoise, an auxiliary to the network's operational activities, whose duties called on her to be a liaison agent, mail box, and hostess, was performing this last role with her customary good humor. Kola was trying to throw off his flu, which he had passed on to her, as she had predicted.

The two of them spent most of their time well wrapped up in bed, he in a bathrobe, she in an old padded dressing gown, without any attempt at intimacy but, equally, without any embarrassing false modesty. They drank toddies, smoked ciga-

rettes, which tasted disgusting, listened alternately to jazz records and the rain pelting down outside, slept, and told each other their dreams. The
pink blouse, which Françoise had draped over the
bedside lamp, kept the room in the same subdued
light day and night. Combined with the heat, the
whiskey, their fevers, and the insistent rain, it produced a surrealist atmosphere, which, fortunately,
led to dreams of more than usual interest.

They shared the bed and their dreams but nothing more. Private lives and past experiences were
never touched on. Françoise made brief excursions,
morning and evening, to buy provisions and the
latest papers, which they searched for any news
item that might justify the general alert. But nothing seemed to be going on that could be construed
as a threat to the network's existence. All they
could do was wait.

Whenever Françoise went out, Kola stood at the
window, hidden by the curtain, to make sure that
she was not being followed, that no one had discovered their hideout. As soon as she was back and
they had combed the papers, they dismissed the
situation from their minds, both of them aware of
the fruitlessness of speculating without any ade-
quate data.

Françoise stubbed out her cigarette in the ash-
tray lying between them on the bed. "Six o'clock.
Time I was off."

She yawned, stretched, and ran a hand through

her tousled hair; then looked disgustedly at the disorder in the room, the bedspread fallen on the carpet, the scattered clothes, the sticky plates and dirty glasses.

"God, what a mess! I must do something about it tomorrow."

Kola was staring at the ceiling, his hands clasped behind his head. Once again, his thoughts had reverted to Dominique, who must be waiting, too, waiting without a clue as to what had happened to him and imagining God knew what. And once again he was reflecting sourly that a profession such as his was irreconcilable with any kind of private life, only with a parallel life, like his antique-dealing, which served to provide cover. For the umpteenth time, he decided to chuck the whole thing, sever his connection with the network, while well aware that it was impossible and that, in fact, he did not really want to; that if he did, he would regard himself as a deserter and end up by hating Dominique for being innocently responsible.

To confide in her was equally impossible. The Service for which he worked had only approved his marriage with a Frenchwoman because they saw it as a clever maneuver, designed to build up his cover while he was working in France, and intended to be "dissolved" when he moved on elsewhere. Genuine feeling of any kind never entered their calculations. They trusted him to deal with

his matrimonial affairs as ruthlessly and compe-
tently as he carried out his various missions.

Unfortunately he had broken the rules by falling headlong in love.

"I'll give myself another half hour," Françoise
was saying. "I can't believe it, but it actually seems
to have stopped raining!"

He turned over to look at her, wondering idly
for the first time whether she knew for whom and
for what cause she was working; or whether she
was another of the mercenaries, content to obey
orders for the sake of the money, without asking
questions.

The front door bell rang. A short, sharp ring.
Kola raised questioning eyebrows toward Françoise, who stared back, petrified, then shook her
head. It could not be Pierre. He always knocked
and, besides, announced his arrival beforehand
with three consecutive telephone calls. Kola
stretched out his arm and turned off the record
player.

The bell rang again, longer this time, and was
followed by the sound of fists hammering on the
door. White-faced, Françoise slipped out of bed.
She had produced a revolver from somewhere and
was gripping it in her right hand. There was no
trace of the young, laughing student about her
now as, in turn, she flashed him a questioning look.
He signed to her to stay where she was, got out of

bed himself, and silently crossed the living room to the small entrance hall.

He could hear a woman's muffled voice coming from the landing outside, "I know you're there! Let me in!" Then, his own name, "Kola! I heard you! Let me in!" It was only then that he recognized the voice as Dominique's. The violent knocking started again. In another minute, she would have the other tenants rushing up to see what was going on. In his dazed state, this was all he could think of. He opened the door.

She stood completely still, staring at him in horrified disbelief, as she took in his ruffled hair, his naked chest under the gaping bathrobe, his bare legs, and his swollen, bloodshot eyes: she could smell the alcohol on his breath. Kola's lips moved soundlessly as he tried to find words and failed. He had been prepared for any eventuality but this. Finally, he heard himself asking with no conscious volition on his part, "How did you find out?"

She brushed past him without answering and, mechanically, he closed the door behind her. She was halfway across the room before he barked out, "Dominique!" and started in pursuit. Then, afraid of Françoise's nervous reaction in her present state of alarm, after the heavy drinking of the past two days, he shouted, "Françoise! It's my wife! Don't . . . !"

Dominique had stopped in the open doorway to the bedroom. Looking over her shoulder, Kola saw that Françoise had got rid of the revolver. She was staring at Dominique, completely at a loss. Dominique's eyes went slowly round the room, dwelling on the rumpled bed, the underclothes on the armchair, the draped lamp, and the record player before finally coming to rest on Françoise.

"How did you know I was here?" Kola asked roughly. "Who gave you this address?"

Beyond speech, Dominique turned around, as if she had seen enough and only wanted to get away. She came face to face with Kola, who barred her path and grabbed her savagely by the wrists.

"Who gave you this address?"

It was probably the first time in his life that he had lost his self-control. Caught up in this farcical scene, which was not of his making and which he could not explain, he was in a blind fury.

"Who told you? Come on! Who told you?"

Dominique managed to break his hold and backed into the bedroom, confronted by a man whom she could scarcely recognize. By now, Françoise had grasped the situation and realized that, for the moment, they must let this woman believe what she thought she saw, while they tried to find out where the leak had occurred; this took precedence over everything. Instinctively, she did what a tart would have done in similar circumstances, turned her back on them, moved over to the window, and pretended to take no further interest in the proceedings.

It all happened in a matter of seconds. She heard Dominique stumble forward with a shrill animal cry of pain, and then the room seemed to explode. She whipped around, suddenly remembering the revolver which she had tossed onto the bed just before Dominique appeared in the doorway.

Kola was toppling forward, his fingers spread out wide in front of him and his mouth open, as though he were about to scream. Dominique was crouching down at the foot of the bed, still pointing the revolver at him. As she rushed forward to snatch it away, Françoise just had time to glimpse Dominique's chalk-white face turning toward her and the jerky movement of her arm before the second bullet struck her full in the chest.

Still gripping the revolver, Dominique raced out of the apartment and down the staircase. A murmur of voices filled the building, doors were flung open, and, from somewhere above her, as metallic and incomprehensible as a tape in reverse, a man's shouts resounded off the walls. On the first floor, an enormously fat woman stood in the doorway of her apartment, gaping. Dominique, panic-stricken enough to fire at random, leveled the revolver at her, and the door slammed shut. The concierge, in a black beret, was holding on to the banisters at the foot of the stairs, craning up. As soon as she came into view, he raised his hands and cringed back into a corner. She ran past him and went on running when she reached the street. People seemed to be leaning from every window, shouting after her. She plunged straight ahead, outdistancing the nonexistent pursuit.

FIVE

She went down one street after another haphazardly, without caring where it led. By now, breath-
lessness had compelled her to slow down to a walking pace, and people had ceased to turn and look
at her. At some point, she had slipped the revolver
into the pocket of her raincoat, and she could feel
it slapping against her thigh. Her memory brought
back the scene in the bedroom in a series of jerky
pictures, like a badly cut film: Kola's furious expression, the untidy bed, the "other woman's" ponytail.
The stain on Kola's bathrobe dissolved into a shot
of the two bodies slumping to the floor, Kola with

his hands outstretched as though he were trying to catch hold of her again, the woman with another stain spreading over her chest as though someone had thrown crimson ink at her.

She began to walk faster and went down the stairs to a Métro station without any particular destination in view. A woman, coming in the opposite direction, paused for a moment to stare at her. Uneasy, Dominique continued on her way for a few more steps, then rushed back up again and entered a bar on the far side of the street.

Edging along the counter, she reached the rest room and locked herself in. Some sense of reality was returning to her, enough, at least, to make her wonder what she was doing there. She thought of telephoning the police or going to the nearest police station to give herself up, but recognized at once that she was incapable of doing it. She would be plunged right back again into the middle of the nightmare.

She took off her raincoat and held it up in front of her at arm's length to make sure that it was not bloodstained, then patted her hair back into some kind of shape. She noticed that her wrists had swollen from Kola's savage grip, but she was not conscious of any pain. All she felt was an indefinable terror.

She put the raincoat on again and leaned against the wall with her eyes closed, fighting to

54

regain her self-control. Outwardly, she must resume an appearance of normality. Studying herself in the mirror before she left, she was astonished to find her reflection little altered from what it had been when she last saw it, seated at her dressing table. She walked back through the bar, with its stuffy smell of beer and damp clothes, past the group at the counter, which broke up to make way for her without giving her a second glance. She half expected an outcry as she emerged into the street but there was no sound beyond the usual steady hum of the traffic.

She started off again, devoid of any emotion now, numbed, carried forward by the automatic reflex of nerves and muscles. She walked along the streets and boulevards, past lighted store windows, threading her way through the crowds without being aware of any of them. Her hands were in her pockets, the right one resting on the butt of the revolver, but the contact brought no recollection of what she had done with it.

She crossed the Seine by the Pont des Arts, and it was like crossing a frontier. Suddenly she had stepped back three years into a country she knew well, where everything that had happened to her since she left had become magically erased. Here, everything was familiar, the buildings, the street lights, the smells, and the small café that she had just passed on her left.

She walked back and went inside, finding a vacant table in a corner of the room, where she ordered tea. She had not returned to it since her marriage, and it was full of new faces, except for the waiter's. When he brought her order, she stared up at him, hoping for a smile or a friendly expression of surprise, but he remained stolidly deadpan. Disappointed, she drank her tea hurriedly and fished in her pocket for money to pay. She came up with a few notes and some loose change, about two hundred francs in all: though it would have meant little to her a few hours ago, it now seemed a small fortune.

Outside in the street again, the weather had turned colder, and her short rest had only accentuated her exhaustion. Her surroundings were as familiar as ever, but they no longer seemed to welcome her. Then she suddenly recognized an old, four-storied house, with tiny windows and wooden balconies, just ahead of her. Hélène lived at the top in one large room, cluttered up with books and fashion sketches; Hélène, who had always been delighted to see her and would feed her and give her a bed for the night without asking questions.

She looked up. The lights were on. Now all she had to do was to whistle a few familiar notes and the key would be thrown down to her. She rounded her lips, whistled the tune softly to herself, and walked on. She had not spoken or written to Hélène for three years, and in the present circumstances, she was hardly an *attractive* guest with whom to land her.

It occurred to her, for the first time, that she was hardly an *attractive* guest with whom to land anyone . . .

By the time the police reached the apartment in the Rue Clauzel, Kola was dead. Françoise, alive but unconscious, was rushed by ambulance to Lariboisière Hospital. Inquiries from the concierge and his wife elicited little information of any value about this new tenant, who had only moved in a few days before and had received no mail. The only unassailable fact to emerge was that the crime had been committed by a woman, but it was impossible to obtain any reliable description of her.

A plastic wallet, obviously new, was found on the dead man. It contained an identity card, made out to Nicolas Balsier, aged forty-six, insurance agent, with an address in the Rue Ramey. His other possessions consisted of three hundred francs in notes, some loose change, a pack of Gitanes with one cigarette left in it, and a dirty handkerchief without initials or laundry marks. Nothing else.

The detective dispatched to the Rue Ramey discovered that Nicolas Balsier was not living at the address shown. Rather more interesting was the fact that no one of that name had ever lived there.

After this, it required only a telephone call to the Préfecture and a ten-minute search of the files to establish that the identity card was a forgery.

At 19:45 hours, Inspector Tarbonel was official-ly placed in charge of the case. He was a solid, even-tempered man in his middle forties with a predilection for English clothes and a deliberately restrained manner to go with them. The pleasure he took in being mistaken for an Anglo-Saxon, which happened from time to time in bars where he was not known, left his colleagues completely baffled. It was, however, a harmless foible, and he had the reputation of being an imaginative and te-nacious officer.

While the police surgeon examined the body and the Identification Squad went about their busi-ness of fingerprinting and photographing, he waited patiently in the living room. Elsewhere in the building, his assistant, Jouffert, was doggedly taking statements from all the tenants who had been at home when the shooting occurred.

The police surgeon, with his hat pulled down over his eyebrows, eventually emerged from the bedroom and headed straight for the front door. On his way, he muttered that death had been vir-tually instantaneous, caused by a bullet fired from a distance of less than ten feet, which had per-forated the aorta, and that he would send in his re-port when he had completed the autopsy. As soon as the technicians had followed, the stretcher bearers came in to remove the body. Tarbonel told them to wait and went into the bedroom, closing the door behind him.

After a quick glance at the crumpled figure on the floor, he drew the covers back over the foot of the bed. The sheets, creased and dirty from cigarette ashes, still retained the vague imprint of two bodies, but there were none of the stains for which he was looking. The glasses, empty whiskey bottle, jammy plates, scattered crumbs, wadded-up balls of Kleenex, and bottle of aspirin, might suggest a number of things, but a love nest was not one of them. It looked to him as if the two victims had been camping there for some time, trying to get rid of colds and doing little else.

He went into the bathroom and poked around. There were no masculine toilet articles, which was not surprising; he had already noticed that the corpse had several days' growth of beard. Though the concierge had not seen him go up, he had probably been in the apartment for two or three days. The setup suggested a hideout, a theory supported to some extent by the false identity card. Back in the bedroom, he bent down over the dead man and studied his face: he would not have put him down as a criminal, but that did not mean a thing. His fingerprints would soon reveal whether or not he had a police record. He stood up again and called in the stretcher bearers.

When they left, he sat down on the bed and

called up the hospital. The young woman had just
been brought down from the operating room.
They had removed a 7.65 caliber bullet from her
lung, and there had been considerable loss of
blood, but she would pull through. Naturally, she
was in no condition to be questioned. Tarbonel
shrugged and hung up.

The doorbell rang. Jouffert had come back to report. Tarbonel disliked him, prejudiced by the
flashy clothes which he regarded as more appro-
priate to a pimp than a police officer, but which
seemed to suit him rather too well.

"Nothing!" Jouffert announced. "The ones who
saw anything clammed up because they didn't
want to get involved, and the ones who didn't see
a damn thing talked their heads off. Nobody seems
to have heard anything, apart from the shots.
They're all agreed it was a woman, but try and get
a description! Tall and dark, short and fair, wearing a fur coat, wearing a white raincoat! Don't
know what gets into 'em! According to the concierge, she was practically a giant, but he's no
higher than a piss-pot himself, and she was waving
a gun at him at the time, so you can guess what
that's worth! He put her age at around thirty-five,
but he hadn't seen her before." He sniffed contemptuously before asking, "What do you make of
it? Usual triangle?"

It could be, but Tarbonel doubted it. Jealous
women, in his experience, did not go about things

quite so ruthlessly, shooting *both* parties. Still, it was always possible . . .

"Better get to work," he said. "Start with the kitchen. Might be something in the garbage can."

Jouffert grimaced, then took off his raincoat and rolled up his sleeves. Tarbonel went downstairs again. In the overheated lodge, smelling strongly of stew, the concierge was giving a graphic description of the affair to two elderly women, no doubt concierges from neighboring buildings, while his wife washed the dishes and interjected comments of her own.

"Who rented the apartment before?" Tarbonel asked abruptly.

The two women scuttled out as if he might be infectious.

"Oh, it hasn't been rented for a long time. It must have been empty for the best part of six months." There was a note of grievance in the concierge's voice, which Tarbonel put down to regret at lost tips. "There's a real estate agent who's supposed to be handling it, but he's asking too much, even if it is furnished. The last person to take it was a professor of some sort, but he didn't stay long, less than a month, I'd say."

Tarbonel jerked a thumb toward the ceiling. "What about her? Lot of boyfriends?"

"We've already told you," the concierge's wife shouted above the clash of saucepans, "she was a foreigner—Swedish or something—and she only moved in five days ago. So what do you expect us to know about her in that time? We never even saw her. The agent must have given her the key, and she slipped straight up, without as much as a word. We thought she'd come over to take some course or other, same as lots of 'em do, and was getting money from home. It's only foreigners nowadays that can afford those prices. How were we to know that she was being kept?"

Tarbonel stayed a short while longer until it was clear that there was nothing to be gleaned from them, then went back upstairs. Jouffert had emptied the garbage can onto the kitchen floor and was now making a list of the contents of the cupboards.

"Nothing there," he said, nodding toward the garbage can. "A few empty cans and bottles and some paper bags. Nothing else."

Tarbonel went into the bedroom again, switched on the record player, and lowered the needle. "Way Down Yonder in New Orleans."

He began examining the dead man's clothes, more interested in "Nicolas Balsier" than in the woman who had survived him. There was a ring at the front door, and he recognized the hoarse voice of Corvin from *France-soir*, drunk as usual. Kicking the bedroom door shut, he left Jouffert to cope.

"Music while you work, eh?" Corvin commented from the living room and gave a bellow of laughter. Tarbonel switched off the record player.

"Balsier's" suit, ready-made and cheap, seemed to be new. Like his underclothes and shoes, it could have been bought at any of Uniprix's branches. They contrasted curiously with the well-cut tweed overcoat which had obviously come from an expensive tailor and which, despite the quality of the cloth, was beginning to show signs of long wear.

The woman's possessions had already been listed and revealed nothing illuminating. Tarbonel piled the dead man's clothes into one of her suitcases and called Jouffert in. It was now 9:10. Two more detectives and another bunch of reporters had arrived.

"Take these things over to the Medical-Legal Institute," he told Jouffert. "Get them to dress him and give him a shave. We'll need photographs for the morning editions. Then, maybe . . ."

He was interrupted by the telephone. He reached it on the second ring, picked up the receiver and pressed it to his ear, without saying anything. Jouffert stood, frozen, with the suitcase in his hand. Conversation in the living room died away.

Tarbonel replaced the receiver. "They've hung up."

He got to the central exchange in the faint hope of tracing the call, but, as he had expected, nothing came of it. The call had been made from a pay phone.

At this particular moment, Dominique was seated in the Vieux Sancerre at Saint-Séverin. The bistro was filled with its usual crowd of hippies and nomads. She had weaved her way through them until she eventually found an empty table. Around her, she caught snatches of conversation in English, German, and Danish. No one showed the remotest interest in his neighbors.

Facing her, by the window, a young man with long, curly hair and an earring in his left ear seemed to be asleep or meditating, his chin buried in the opening of a huge sheepskin jacket. Beside him an olive-skinned girl with a pretty, grubby face, was absentmindedly stroking a kitten curled up in a ball on her lap.

A bearded man in a parka came up to their table and asked, in French, "When are you off?"

The young man looked up and yawned. "Eleven."

"Going far?"

"Antibes." It was the girl who answered. "We'll be staying there for a little while. A friend's promised to put us up on a boat."

The bearded man ignored her and continued to address her companion. "Going by truck?"

"Yes. I had to fork out thirty francs, but hitching's too tough for Maria at the moment."

The bearded man raised his hand a few inches in a gesture of farewell and moved on.

Dominique leaned forward. "Can I come with you?"

The girl peered at her dispassionately. The kitten, snuggling up against the swollen stomach protruding from her unbuttoned coat, was purring like a boiling kettle.

The young man asked, without interest, "Got any money?"

Dominique nodded and joined them at their table, holding out the pack of cigarettes that she had just bought. She thought of offering them sandwiches as well, but they were no longer paying any attention to her. Immersed in their own secret thoughts, the three of them sat there until it was time to leave.

SIX

Pierre had called from a pay phone in the Saint-Lazare Métro station. If all had been well, Françoise would not have answered, and he would have hung up after the third ring. This was his identification signal. After that, he would have called back immediately, Françoise would have lifted the receiver at the first ring and waited four seconds before breathing into the mouthpiece; an indication that Kola was with her and everything in order. Then, at the last moment, she would have told Kola where to meet him: the 93 bus stop, opposite the Cour de Rome. A simple matter of routine.

When he had heard the receiver lifted on his second ring, his stomach had turned. For a second he had nursed the hope that she had answered automatically in a fit of absentmindedness and had expected her to speak. But breathing was plainly audible at the other end, breathing much too heavy to be hers. He had drawn the inevitable conclusion.

He hung up, left the telephone booth, and walked rapidly away. A man of fifty-three, on the short side but broad-shouldered, he was dressed like a bank clerk. There was nothing about his face, with its red-veined nose, large graying mustache, and horn-rimmed glasses, to make anyone give it a second glance. He might have been just another family man hurrying to catch a suburban train back to the wife and kids, scarcely any more harassed and tired than those around him.

He bought a late edition and went up into the concourse of the main station to read the headlines. The network had been combing the papers for the last few days without finding anything that seemed to relate to its existence. There was nothing of significance in the evening paper, either. So if something had happened in the Rue Clauzel, it must have happened in the last few hours, unless the police had muzzled the press.

He had been informed of Kola's return as soon as the latter had contacted Françoise. He regretted now that he had allowed three days to pass without having made discreet inquiries to confirm that all was well at the apartment. It was apparent that the original alarm, which had sent members of the network into hiding, had been a false one, and excessive precautions had led him into an error of omission.

But there could be nothing false about the present alarm. Pierre folded his paper, went into another telephone booth, and rang up Marius, the network's resident agent in Paris. Twenty minutes later they met in the Place de la Madeleine, outside Cook's.

"Something's happened in the Rue Clauzel," Pierre said as soon as they had started walking up the boulevard. "It's in the ninth, beyond the Place Saint-Georges. Number Thirty-seven. Girl called Françoise Oscarsen and a man called Nicolas Balsier."

He had to tilt his head up toward Marius, who was considerably taller and looked like a Dutch professor, with his red hair, pale, freckled skin, and broad, intellectual forehead. Marius listened attentively without asking any questions. The two names meant nothing to him, and he had no idea whether they belonged to members of the network or the other side. Like all Pierre's associates, he adhered strictly to the policy of watertight compartments, in which no one knew more than was absolutely necessary: it offered them their best chance of survival.

Pierre went on, "I want you to go up there and scout around. Drop into the cafés, and see what you can pick up. But just listen. Don't ask questions. And meet me again at the Select in Montparnasse at eleven."

Marius nodded and went off toward the Métro. Pierre spent the next hour arranging for a new warning to be relayed through the network. He was uncomfortably aware that some, at least, of his subordinates would regard him as a fussy alarmist and might even suspect that he was beginning to lose his nerve. But they had no precise knowledge of the danger involved, and, in any case, their own safety was not immediately threatened. He himself was the one in trouble if Kola and Françoise had been picked up since both of them knew him. He had few doubts about Kola, but Françoise, under pressure, would almost certainly talk in the end.

Before keeping his appointment at the Select he ate a sandwich and drank a glass of beer at the counter of a café, enjoying them both, despite his nagging anxiety. Over the years, he had learned to relish the minor pleasures of life, whatever the circumstances. At the same time, one part of his

69

mind revolved around the microfilms. He would have given a lot to know whether Kola had managed to tuck them away somewhere safe.

Marius turned up promptly at 11:00, and they immediately left together.

"The girl and the other character got themselves shot," Marius reported. "There were still a couple of police cars outside Number Thirty-seven when I passed. The whole neighborhood was buzzing with it. It seems they were shot in one of the apartments by a woman."

"Anyone know who she was?" Pierre asked, without revealing his eagerness.

"No. She got away. The general theory is that she was the man's wife, caught him with his mistress."

Pierre stopped, took out his handkerchief, and wiped his glasses.

"Did she kill them?" His voice was still expressionless.

"She killed the man. The girl was taken to the hospital."

Pierre slowly replaced his glasses and moved on again. "Which hospital?"

"Someone mentioned Lariboisière, but I think it was just a guess. It's the only hospital they've heard of in Montmartre."

Pierre walked the next hundred yards in silence. Taking a cigar from the inside pocket of his jacket, he stuck it in his mouth without lighting it. Finally he said reflectively, "Chances are that it was Lariboisière, all the same."

"We could call up and find out."

Pierre eyed him coldly. He did not appreciate suggestions from subordinates. And in any case, there was no effective action to be taken that night.

"Was she badly wounded? I suppose no one knew?"

"They said she was unconscious when she was put in the ambulance, but that doesn't mean . . ."

Pierre broke in. "This is what you'll have to do, first thing tomorrow. Buy a bunch of roses from some florist where you're not known . . . No, not roses; something less showy. Carnations . . . and tear the shop's name off the wrapping paper. Then meet me outside the Pigalle Métro at nine fifteen. Wear a dark suit and get hold of a cloth cap— something that'll make you look like a delivery man. Get the idea?" He gave Marius's arm a gentle squeeze and left him without waiting for an answer.

As soon as he came across an empty taxi, he jumped in and told the driver to take him to Saint-Germain. The drugstore there was the only place open at this time of night where he could buy a bottle of toilet water. On the way, he lit his cigar and weighed the situation. Unless her wound had been superficial, which was unlikely, Françoise would not come to from anesthesia for several hours, which meant that she could not be questioned till the following morning, though, admittedly, the police rarely showed much consideration in cases of this kind.

But even assuming the worst, facing the possibility that she was being questioned at this actual moment, she would not talk. Not yet. He knew her well enough to be confident that she would be able to hold out during the first interrogation, use her physical weakness as an excuse for not answering—if necessary, faint. And that was all he required of her. For the time being . . .

He bought a bottle of Dior 'Eau Fraîche' at the drugstore. All that remained now was to drop it in on Herman, who lived nearby in the Ile Saint-Louis. It would take Herman only a couple of hours to do what was necessary.

There were still two problems to be solved. The identity of the woman who had fired the shots and had obviously been able to find out Françoise's address, the network's most recently acquired hideout: this was a matter of extreme urgency. Secondly, the location of the films that Kola had brought back from Lyon.

But for the moment, Françoise took precedence over everything else. First things first . . .

Tarbonel called the hospital at seven in the morning. Franoçise Oscarsen had not yet fully recovered consciousness, but she was expected to do so at any moment. There was no question of him seeing her even for a few minutes before evening, and he might well have to wait till the following day.

All that was known of her was contained in the brief typewritten summary lying on the desk in front of him. Her passport, in the name of Oscarsen, was genuine; she was domiciled in Sweden, and her address there had been verified; she had been living in France for the past two and a half years after several short periods of residence in Germany and England; at one time a member of a troupe of acrobatic dancers, she seemed recently to have become a free-lance contributor to various Scandinavian magazines; her residence permit was in order; and she had formerly rented an apartment in the Rue Lamarck.

Tarbonel picked up one of the photographs of Nicolas Balsier, clothed and shaven, and set out for the Rue Lamarck.

Françoise opened her eyes at 8:20. She had been put in a private room at the request of the police and was receiving intensive care. The special nurse immediately notified the duty doctor that her patient had recovered consciousness, and after examining her, he decided that she no longer required intravenous feeding. She went to sleep again at once.

At 9:30 the nurse's aide brought up a large

bunch of red carnations and a small parcel, which had been left in the patient's name at the reception desk. The special nurse, a fat, cheerful woman from Toulouse, arranged the flowers in a vase and placed them on the bedside table with a little nod of approval. These little attentions always had a beneficial effect on patients' morale.

When her innate curiosity led her to unwrap the parcel, she was even more impressed by the anonymous donor's good taste. Flowers and Dior toilet water were a considerable improvement over the bottles of red wine, which were the customary postoperation gifts to patients in the public wards. She was almost as pleased as if she herself had been the recipient. No doubt the absence of a card meant that none was necessary: the young woman would recognize the sender as soon as she woke up.

The nurse had been told the bare outlines of the drama and had since formed a clear mental picture of the missing characters: the wealthy, suave businessman, who had been "keeping" her patient, and his fat dowdy wife, who had reacted so impetuously, though understandably, on finding them together. Now, on the evidence of the presents, it looked as though she could add a devoted boyfriend, prepared to forgive all. A sentimental smile spread over her face at the thought of him. It was like a story in *True Romances*, better in fact than most of them, since they rarely contained so much action, and the young woman belonged to a vastly different world from that of the good-for-nothings, knifed in drunken brawls, with whom she so often had to deal.

In her state of euphoria, she decided to wake up her patient. It could not do any harm, quite the contrary, since the doctor had been completely satisfied with her condition. Scarcely any fever and a pulse that, though weak, was almost back to normal. She bent over the bed and began gently patting her cheeks. From past experience, she knew that the young man had provided just what women liked to find on coming out of an anesthetic: flowers as reassurance that somebody loved them and something cool and fragrant to put on their foreheads. After that, they went happily back to sleep. It was better than any medicine.

She took the stopper out of the bottle and sniffed its contents with her eyes closed. Personally, she would have preferred a stronger perfume, but it was pleasant and refreshing. She poured some on a handkerchief and placed it on Françoise's forehead. As she did so, she felt suddenly dizzy, as though a flash bulb had gone off in the room, causing her to see everything double. It lasted for only a fraction of a second and reminded her that it had been some time since she had had her blood pressure checked; or it might have been due to fatigue after too long a period on night duty. In any case, she was now right as rain again.

Françoise sighed. The nurse added a little more toilet water to the handkerchief and held it under her patient's nose, gently dabbing at the perspiration on her upper lip.

"Smells nice, dear, doesn't it?"

Due to her lung injury, Françoise's breathing was very shallow—little gasps for air that scarcely inflated her chest. Presently, she took a slightly deeper breath, and the nurse gave a smile of satisfaction. This clearly meant that the young woman was recovering her sense of smell. Then, suddenly, Françoise's body seemed to contract and, a second later, equally suddenly, to relax. Now her breathing had stopped altogether.

The concierge at the building in the Rue Lamarck had read the morning papers and was half expecting a visit from the police. Tarbonel found her voluble but not enlightening . . .

Yes, the "victim" had rented an apartment in the building, a small, furnished one on the top floor. A quiet girl who kept to herself. No, the concierge didn't remember any of her friends in particular. She'd had visitors from time to time—it would have been odd, at her age, if she hadn't—but she hadn't gone in for noisy parties or anything like that. There'd probably been more men than women, but that didn't make her a prostitute, did it? Of course, Swedes . . . Yes, she'd received letters, the same as everyone else, some of them from abroad. Never any trouble, always pleasant to everyone, but you couldn't call her gabby, exactly. Didn't throw her money around but wasn't stingy, either. The concierge didn't know why she'd left; it was none of her business. Yes, now that Tarbonel mentioned it, she *had* left rather suddenly, but no doubt she'd had her reasons or it might have been for no reason at all, just a whim. Young women nowadays . . . The concierge was a concierge not a mother-confessor. She didn't wait around for people to confide in her.

Tarbonel produced the photograph.

Yes, the concierge had an idea that she'd seen the man going up to the apartment: she'd thought so when she'd first seen the photo in the *Parisien*. It was the same photograph, wasn't it? But she couldn't be sure; she wouldn't like to swear to it, if Tarbonel understood what she meant . . .

He left Jouffert behind to make the usual routine inquiries from the tenants and local shopkeepers and drove to the offices of the Police Judiciaire. He got there at ten o'clock and was immediately informed of Françoise Oscarsen's death, a death that could not be attributed to her injuries. Detectives had already been sent to the hospital to investigate. Tarbonel hurried off to join them.

He found several doctors in the private room, grouped around Françoise's rigid body. One of them pointed out her purplish-blue lips and mottled face, sure signs of poisoning, then nodded toward the restoppered bottle, standing on a nearby table, alongside the flowers and the handkerchief, which had been placed in a metal container.

"Left for her this morning at the reception desk. Seemed quite normal, and as there weren't any special instructions ..."

"Was it the toilet water?" Tarbonel broke in.

The doctor shrugged, and an older man answered for him. "Probably. We'll know for certain when it's been analyzed. In any case, the nurse can't be held responsible. She was merely carrying out her duties."

"A bit too efficiently," Tarbonel said dryly.

The nurse was being questioned by two detectives in one of the administration offices. Slumped in a chair, with tears pouring down her fat cheeks, she was making no attempt to justify herself. As Tarbonel came in, she was saying for the fourth time, "I should never have touched it!"

He sized her up in a quick glance, asked a few questions of his own, and told the men to let her go as soon as she had signed her statement.

"Find out anything from reception?"

"Precious little." The senior detective looked resigned. "They say some character dropped the flowers and parcel in around nine thirty this morning. Didn't pay much attention to him. He could have been a delivery man or someone's chauffeur.

One of the girls noticed that he was freckled. Apart from that ..."

The analysis disclosed that the toilet water contained several centigrams of a toxic substance, absorbable by inhalation and, to a lesser extent, by osmosis.

"It dates back to the Borgias," the laboratory technician informed an unappreciative Tarbonel. "The man who doctored the stuff knew his dosages all right. He put in just the right amount for the combined effects, particularly on the face, to be instantaneous."

Pierre read of Françoise's death in the first edition of *France-soir*. She had been eliminated even earlier than he had expected. It had been a hard decision to make, and though his planning had produced the required result, there was no satisfaction to be gained from it. He merely felt depressed and angry. But had she lived, she would have had no plausible story to give the police, and she knew enough to constitute a threat to the existence of the whole network. He had done no more than comply with the ruthless rules of the game in which they were all involved.

An ex-naval officer, he commanded the network as he would have commanded a submarine in enemy waters, keeping submerged for long periods, surfacing occasionally to make a strike, and immediately disappearing again. When the ship was in danger, all watertight bulkheads had to be closed, even if someone got caught in one of the flooded compartments.

Among the members of the network, there were a few dedicated militants like himself, who knew exactly for whom they were working. Kola had belonged to this small number. The remainder were mercenaries, paid to accept, once and for all, the explanations originally given them without prying further. Like Françoise Oscarsen. The risks were the same for everybody, the only difference being that those in the second category were unaware of the full extent of them.

He folded the paper and stuffed it into his pocket. He could count on comparative safety only for as long as the police failed to identify and pick up the woman who had fled from the scene of the crime. And her identity might not pose much of a problem. It was possible that he would have deduced it, himself, by evening.

On leaving Herman the night before, he had telephoned the Krestowiczes' apartment in the Avenue Mozart solely to find out whether there was anyone there to answer. There had been no reply then or when he had rung up again early that morning and at 10:00. If this merely meant that Kola's wife was out of town, she would be bound to recognize her husband's photograph in one or another of the papers, despite the false name, and learn of his death. She would then naturally contact the police, a fact that would be reported in the press later in the day.

But if no such news item appeared, it would be reasonable to conclude that it had been Dominique Krestowicz herself who had shot her husband and Françoise. At an address that she should have known nothing about. This left a wide field open for speculation on just how much else she had managed to find out ...

Pierre was not the only one to have telephoned the Krestowiczes' apartment. When Dominique had failed to come back to her after two hours, Laura had called her up and tried again later that night. It had finally occurred to her that her friend might be in no mood to talk to her and she had decided to drop in on her early next day.

The morning papers, full of the drama in the Rue Clauzel, caused her to change her mind. When she read the name Nicolas Balsier underneath the photograph, she was shaken to the core. Since Tarbonel had not seen fit to reveal to the press that it was an alias, she thought for a moment that she had been responsible for a ghastly mistake. Then reason reasserted itself: it had unquestionably been Kola whom she had followed; consequently it must be Kola who had been killed, no matter what name appeared in the paper.

Not without a certain pleasurable excitement,

she supposed that it was her duty to tell the police what she knew of the affair and went to the telephone. But she did not dial. After all, it was a pretty sordid crime, and André would strongly disapprove of her being even remotely connected with it. Much better to lie low. She did not *have* to have read the papers. She hurriedly packed a few clothes in a suitcase and went off to spend a few days with her sister in the country.

Once she had gotten over her first shock and was able to consider the matter calmly, she managed to persuade herself that *basically* she bore no responsibility whatever for what had happened. If every wife who discovered that her husband was cheating on her felt impelled to commit murder . . .

She determined to erase all recollection of her friendship with Dominique from her mind. When she had first picked her up, she had had no idea that she would turn out so unsophisticated and illbred . . .

The employee on duty at the general delivery counter had read the newspapers, too, and consequently had learned of Nicolas Balsier's murder. The name rang a bell, having become automatically registered on her mind over the last three days as a result of having seen it each time she ran through the mail in the B pigeonhole.

She found the letter in question and took it in to the postmaster, who promptly got in touch with the police. As soon as it reached Tarbonel, he opened it, extracted the baggage claim, and headed for the Gare de Lyon, where he picked up Kola's suitcase.

Its contents were examined at the Police Judiciare offices. Tarbonel, who had high hopes of what they might yield, was disappointed: there was nothing among them to identify the bag's owner, apart, perhaps, from the camera and two rolls of film. These were sent to the police laboratory.

At 3:30 Tarbonel received instructions to stop all further press releases. And the laboratory did not inform him what the films had disclosed.

The enlarged prints had been rushed to Régnier, the Chief Superintendent. The first page of the photographed documents carried LICOM's heading. Régnier immediately asked Tarbonel for a complete summary of the case. Once he had read it through, he requested an interview with the Minister of Defense, which was granted at once.

At 4:20 two men, strangers to members of the P.J., walked straight through to the Police Commissioner's office. They had a nondescript appearance, as unremarkable as that of the hundreds of travelers, seen but not noticed, in hotel foyers and airport bars. It would have been difficult to determine either their age or their nationality.

At 4:45 Tarbonel was invited to join them and requested to give a complete account of the whole affair down to the smallest, even seemingly irrelevant, detail. On conclusion, he was asked a number of terse, searching questions.

Three quarters of an hour later, the two strangers left, taking with them all the documents and exhibits relating to the case.

From then on, Tarbonel's role was reduced to that of a mere extra. Though he still remained in charge, as far as the press and public were concerned, Special Services had, in fact, assumed full control. The date was January 21.

SEVEN

At about the same time that afternoon, the truck carrying Dominique and her two companions as passengers was approaching Avignon. Loaded with cheese for Nice, it was long past its best days and extremely slow.

Dominique had fallen asleep almost as soon as she had installed herself in the back, wedged in a small corridor between the stacks of packing cases. Maria had sat down on the floor beside her, leaning against her, while the kitten, superbly indifferent to the swaying and jolting, prowled around, sniffing at the cargo and returning from time to time to perch on his mistress's shoulder. The young man, Tom, had gotten in the cab next to the driver.

It was snowing when they reached the Morvan, and Dominique was awakened by icy water dripping down on her from the tarpaulin cover. Maria merely moaned in her sleep and huddled still closer against her. At 3:00 in the morning, the truck stopped, and Tom raised the back flap to ask if they wanted to get out and have some coffee. Reluctant to wake Maria, who was now sleeping almost across her, Dominique signaled no. Ten minutes later, they started off again.

Dominique began to feel as though she had solidified into a block of ice; the cold spread up from her ankles through her whole body. Though she was scarcely aware of it anymore, she found it impossible to get to sleep again. She remained in a sort of torpor, too numbed to think, her mind merely registering the various discomforts: cramp in her thighs, a pain in her back, the corner of a packing case stabbing her between the shoulder blades each time they rounded a corner, and the unappetizing smell of the cheese mingling with that of Maria's unwashed body.

At daybreak they made another stop for a snack. This time, unable to bear her weight any longer, Dominique woke up Maria, and they stumbled out into the road, bleary-eyed, astonished to find the two men wide awake, smoking and talking. There

were a number of huge trucks parked outside the
café, from which drivers were emerging, buttoning
up their leather jackets. When they got inside, the
bleak room, smelling of stale cigarette smoke and
rum, was empty. After drinking scalding coffee,
eating hard-boiled eggs, and providing the kitten
with a saucer of milk, they set out again.

They made a third stop about midday, when Tom
had brought sandwiches and bottles of milk to the
truck. After that, the two young women dozed off
by fits and starts until there had been a sudden
softness in the air, as though they had crossed a
frontier leaving the cold zone behind. Then,
shoulder to shoulder, comforted by the comparative warmth, they had fallen into a deep sleep.

That morning, a number of people who were ac-
quainted with Nicolas Krestowicz were shocked
when they opened their newspapers and saw the
photograph of the man murdered in the Rue Clauzel. They included some of the tenants in the
apartment house, the Krestowiczes' cleaning
woman, the proprietor of the garage where Kola
kept his car, and several of his clients. It could, of
course, only be a chance resemblance, since the
victim's name was Balsier, but the features were
curiously similar, and so were their Christian
names . . .

When the cleaning woman rang the bell as usual
at 9:00, there was no answer. This was surprising

because when Madame Krestowicz wanted to sleep late, as she had the day before, she left the key in the service door. The cleaning woman rang again several times, then went downstairs to ask the concierge whether Madame had gone away. As far as the concierge knew, she had not, though now she came to think of it, she had seen Madame Krestowicz go out on the previous afternoon and had not seen her return. Perhaps with her husband away on one of his trips, she had decided to spend the night with a friend. A woman friend, of course . . .

The cleaning woman went home, disgruntled, wondering whether she would get paid for the hours she had wasted. It was only some time later, after she had settled down to read her newspaper and been struck by the photograph's uncanny like-ness to Monsieur Krestowicz, that she began to add one thing to another. To start with, there was the photograph; then there was Madame going away like that without letting her know; and third-ly, there was the curious state in which she had found the apartment during the last few days, glasses smelling of liquor, and the contents of a brandy bottle disappearing with extraordinary ra-pidity.

All the same, she decided to do nothing about it. It was a ticklish situation, and if she interfered, her good intentions might not be appreciated. But she brooded on it all afternoon when she was out on another job, and at 5:30 she called the apartment because it did begin to look ...

At 6:00 she was in the Sixteenth District's police station, tactfully drawing the duty sergeant's attention to the matter. She could get no answer from her employer's apartment; her employer had never mentioned that she might be going away; so she could not help wondering whether, perhaps, there had been an accident. The sergeant was inquisitive by nature and profession. He assured her that he fully understood her anxiety in view of the circumstances: it was only natural and did her credit. And he proceeded to draw her out. Relieved to share her worries with someone else, particularly with a sympathetic and good-looking man, she went on to mention the photograph in the paper.

The sergeant immediately asked her to wait and went off to report to the superintendent, who, in turn, reported to the P.J. Twenty minutes later Tarbonel turned up, had a brief chat with the cleaning woman, and took her away in his car.

At 7:15 the cleaning woman formally identified the body lying on the marble slab as that of Nicolas Krestowicz, the husband of her employer.

Under the new arrangement, Tarbonel's duties were confined to passing on the information to the right quarters.

Pierre had gone back to his own small bachelor apartment, where he had spent the whole afternoon. The living room was littered with stamp albums and catalogs; he had been examining and rearranging his collection. It was an occupation that absorbed all his attention and could be relied on to restore his peace of mind.

At 4:30 he put the albums away and set about composing and coding his message. When he had finished, his neat, closely written figures filled half a quarto-sized sheet of paper. Transmission was set for 5:30, French time.

Going into the bedroom, he crossed to the window, which looked down on a small courtyard and faced a cracked concrete wall. After closing the shutters, he switched on a lamp and took a screwdriver out of the chest of drawers. He then knelt down and raised three strips of the parquet. From the hiding place underneath, he drew out the components of a small transmitter, which he assembled with the speed of long practice. Its keys were linked to a miniature tape recorder.

Turning on a transistor radio on the bedside table, broadcasting dance music, he plugged the transmitter in, sat down on the floor with the sheet of figures in front of him, and began manipulating the keys. The tape slowly unwound while the transmitter remained switched off. When he had recorded the message, he rewound the tape and concentrated on his watch. As 5:30 came up, he switched the transmitter on, pressed a button on the recorder, and the tape unwound again in a flash. The whole transmission had taken four seconds, well within the time necessary for anyone to get a trace on the set by a direction finder.

A quarter of an hour later, he plugged in the receiving set, put on the headphones, and got an acknowledgment of his message on the same frequency. Dismantling the apparatus, he restored it to its hiding place, relaid the parquet, and lit a cigar. At 9:00 he would have his reply.

The dance music began to get on his nerves. He turned the dial till a symphony orchestra came in. Then, with the cigar clamped between his teeth and his over-long dressing gown flapping around his ankles, he went into the kitchen to make some tea. When the kettle boiled, he poured himself a cup, carried it back to the bedroom, and stretched out on the bed. Listening to the music with his eyes half closed, he alternately sipped the tea and nibbled at the lump of sugar held in his other hand. His cigar slowly went out on the marble surface of the bedside table.

At 10:00 Pierre made a telephone call from a booth in a café near the Ecole Militaire and arranged a rendezvous outside the Etoile Métro in half an hour. The man who met him there was in his middle thirties, with a large, round face on which an expression of deep melancholy sat incongruously. They fell into step without greeting each other and began walking down the Avenue Foch. It was only after they had gone a hundred yards that Pierre broke the silence.

"Fedor Alexandrovich . . ."

The other man gave him a quick look, astounded to hear himself addressed by his real name. It was a harmless enough breach of security in their present surroundings but particularly unexpected, coming from Pierre. But he had no time to dwell on it, for Pierre, in a low, expressionless voice, staring down at the pavement in front of him, had embarked on an account of the whole operation since its inception: the application of the LICOM formulas photographed at Lyon; Kola's return to Paris; his enforced wait at Françoise's apartment; and his murder by the unknown woman. When he went on to detail the planning that had led up to Françoise's death—omitting Marius's name—Fedor had a sudden feeling of revulsion. He opened his mouth to ask a question, but Pierre stopped him with a gentle pressure on his arm.

"Krestowicz was married," he continued. "And right now it looks as if it was his wife who shot him. God knows why! Your guess is as good as mine. It could be that she was retained by one of the other services and was sent to take the films away from him. Or if he slipped up somewhere, she may have grown suspicious of those trips of his and had him watched. Or, for that matter, she may have managed to follow him to the apartment herself. It doesn't really matter. The point is that she obviously knows too much. I don't say it amounts to a lot, but we've no way of finding out, and we can't afford to count on it.

"I reported to Control, asked them for instructions, and sent them her description, the one Krestowicz gave me when he married her. We always ask for a description and photograph in those cases. They'll be relaying the description to all our other networks here—and everywhere else, I imagine. In addition, they're providing two torpedoes to work under me, who'll go into action as soon as there's a trace of her. Unless the police are holding back on their press releases, they haven't got anywhere so far. Krestowicz hasn't been identified yet, and no one's come across the films. So let's hope we can eliminate her before they pick her up and make her talk."

"Why are you telling me all this?" Fedor asked uneasily.

They had reached the Porte Dauphine. Turning around, they began walking back the way they had come.

"Because I want you to realize exactly what we're up against, why Control takes such a serious view of it."

"Was Krestowicz . . ."

"He was a Pole. He used his own name as part of his cover—very unusual, but they thought it would be an advantage in his case because, officially, he was a defector."

"That wasn't what I wanted to know!" Fedor's voice was tinged with exasperation. "You're telling me far too much. It's pointless . . . and dangerous."

"Sorry!" Pierre slowly drew a hand across his forehead. "The fact is, I can't get Krestowicz out of my mind. I can't forget I was responsible for him—his assignments, his whole way of life, and now, up to a point, his death. If only I'd contacted him a few hours earlier instead of being distracted by that damn false alarm, he'd still be alive and we'd have the films safely in our hands." His expression hardened. "There's no getting away from it, I'm responsible for both deaths—his and Oscarsen's. Two first-class agents, who'll be damn difficult to replace. And we may have lost scientific information that would have put us way ahead, industrially and defensively. I received a reprimand, that goes without saying, and orders to make the maximum effort to recover the films."

Fedor listened with growing amazement. Self-criticism, uttered coldly and precisely, was a familiar feature of state trials at home, but it was completely alien to Pierre, who never disclosed either thoughts or feelings even to the closest of his associates. It was as though he had been drawing up a personal balance sheet. But the next moment he seemed to put it all behind him, and his voice recovered its normal crispness.

"They want us to try the Rue Clauzel apartment first. Logical enough, I suppose. Krestowicz may have hidden the films there as soon as he arrived. The question is, where? The only thing is to search it from top to bottom, using some imagination. Try to think along the lines he did. If the woman didn't manage to get hold of them, they may still be there. There's another possibility, of course. The police may have found them and be keeping it quiet. In that case, they'll be expecting us to turn up, and they'll have laid a trap. It's a hell of a risk, whichever way you look at it because whether they've found the films or not, Oscarsen's death will have made them realize that there's more to the whole business than they thought at first, so they're liable to have laid a trap anyway."

"Is this where I come in?" Fedor asked abruptly.

"Afraid so. Personally, I have a hunch that the films are no longer in the apartment, if they ever were, but I have nothing to go on. If I'm right, you'll be risking your neck for nothing. But the orders left no option."

"Did they nominate me, specifically?"

"No, they always leave the choice to me. I picked you because you're the best man we have."

Fedor's lips twitched. "Isn't that a bit wasteful ... in the circumstances?"

"From an operational point of view, yes. But

that doesn't seem to weigh with them. I suggested I should go myself, since we can't send one of the mercenaries, but they turned it down."

"Why can't we send—?"

"Because of the special instructions." Pierre rushed his words. "The operative mustn't be taken alive. We couldn't count on a mercenary if it came to that."

After a short pause, Fedor asked, "When?"

"Later tonight. Three thirty. The usual precautions. No papers or anything else on you by which you can be identified. Nothing, in fact, but this . . ." Pierre took a small, rolled-up tool kit out of his pocket and handed it over. "I don't imagine you'll have much difficulty with the lock. If you haven't found anything by five, give up. But if you do strike it lucky, come straight back and drop the films here . . ." He led Fedor up a narrow passage and pointed to a litter basket. "The address is Thirty-seven. The apartment is on the fourth floor."

He felt in his pocket again, produced a small capsule covered in transparent plastic, and dropped it into Fedor's palm. "Keep it in your mouth all through the operation. Afterward, too, till you're certain you aren't being tailed. Under your tongue is the best place. The covering's hard and insoluble. It needs a strong bite to get through it."

Fedor gave a glimmer of a smile. "Suppose I swallow it by mistake?"

Pierre glanced at him and recognized the joke for what it was: an exorcism against fear. He forced himself to smile back. "You won't be charged with wasting valuable material. Gastric juices have no effect on it. We'll just expect you to return it. In due course."

He had answered in Russian. It was the first time that Fedor had heard him use their common language. He tossed the capsule up, caught it in his palm, and slipped it into his pocket.

At that very moment, the rotary presses were churning out the news of the identification of the corpse from the Rue Clauzel. "Antique Dealer Nicolas Krestowicz, alias Nicolas Balsier, Slain by Unknown Woman in Mistress's Flat. Was He Living Double Life?"

There was no mention yet of Dominique's name. Though the police still issued press releases, behind the scenes Special Services were carefully censoring their contents.

After questioning the cleaning woman at considerable length, one of the two men to whom Tarbonel had handed over the investigation called on Percy Lawson, the employee in the antique shop, at his small two-room apartment. Since Percy had a low opinion of French newspapers and never read one, it was not until then that he heard of his employer's death. Once he had gotten over the shock, he, too, was asked to identify the body.

The man from Special Services who questioned him as unconcernedly as if murder were a commonplace affair elicited little useful information. It was not that the willowy, fair-haired Percy was reticent: on the contrary, irresistibly attracted by his visitor, whose sympathetic, understanding manner was in striking contrast to his tough, deeply lined face, he babbled away with the greatest willingness. But it gradually emerged that he had only been working at the shop for a matter of three months and knew nothing of Krestowicz's activities outside business hours.

Confronted by the rows of drawers in the morgue, Percy promptly fainted. He was eventually brought to, and supported on each side while he viewed the body. He was driven back to his apartment by the man from Special Services. On the way, at his request, they stopped at a bar and he drank two double whiskeys. After gulping down the first, he suddenly recollected Dominique's various telephone calls, inquiring whether anything had been heard of her husband at the shop.

"The last one was yesterday afternoon. She rang up in the morning, too. And once or twice the day before. I felt ever so sorry for her. She sounded in a terrible way."

"No call today?"

"No, as a matter of fact, she . . ." Percy's voice trailed off. His eyes wandered around the room. Then he cleared his throat and said thoughtfully, "It does seem a bit odd . . ."

The man from Special Services, who was called Coster and loathed whiskey, waited for Percy to start on his second one before producing a photograph from his pocket and slipping it across the table.

"Know her?"

It was a glossy print of Françoise Oscarsen, probably taken when she was still with the troupe, which Tarbonel had found among her things and included in his file. Percy shook his head.

"No, I've never seen her. But if Krestowicz had a girl friend, he wouldn't have brought her to the shop. He was all business, there. No time for anyone but customers."

He took a large swig of whiskey, flushed, and suddenly blurted out, "You're so . . . I mean, I'd never have taken you for a policeman!"

It was a few seconds before Coster grasped what lay behind the remark. Percy's pale-blue eyes were searching his face and he was breathing rapidly, as though he had been running. A kindly man, Coster gave him a friendly smile and paid the bill.

After dropping Percy, he headed for the Avenue

Mozart. He did not expect to find anything there that would throw much light on Krestowicz. But it was the wife, Dominique, in which he was interested for the moment.

EIGHT

They had reached Antibes at 10:30 in the evening. The truck driver had dropped them on the far side of the town and driven on, after pointing out the way to the harbor. An icy mistral that had been blowing for the last hour enveloped them as they got out. Pale and grubbier than ever, Maria gestured toward her stomach. "Anyway, he knew how to hang on!" She gave a nervous titter and tucked the kitten inside her coat. "So did he. Hope they find it worth it."

Dominique stayed with them. At the last stop, without inquiring into her plans, Tom had casually remarked that he was sure his friend would be able to put her up on the boat for the night. Her thanks had seemed to surprise him as though she had suddenly broken into an unknown language.

They walked together along the deserted quays beside a forest of bobbing masts, to the accompaniment of creaking hawsers and the scraping of gangways against the stone. As they passed each sailing vessel, they bent down to read the name on its stern, hunting for the *Andromeda*. The wind struck them with the concentrated force of a plane's jet stream.

When they had covered the entire harbor without finding the *Andromeda*, they fought their way back to an old fishing boat, hauled up onto the first quay they had searched. Huddled down on its floorboards, they listened impassively to the whistling wind and the various unfamiliar sounds from the surrounding yachts.

It was only as she rubbed her numbed hands up and down the outside of her coat to warm them that Dominique became aware that the revolver was gone. She had no idea as to how long it had been missing. In her exhausted state she had failed to notice that its weight was no longer pressing against her thigh. Glancing at her companions, she wondered whether Maria had taken it when she had appeared to be fast asleep across her in the truck; or Tom, when they had been walking and stumbling against each other just recently on the quay.

She surreptitiously ran her hand down the lining of her pocket. They had, at least, left her her money. She could still feel the notes there. But this might only be because the gun had been easier to extract than the notes.

Now she began wondering why she was so shocked by the discovery of her loss. Certainly it was not because she had lost the gun. She had no further use for it. Perhaps it was because, in stealing from her, they had rejected her, made it plain that to them she was just a stranger. But then on reflection, what did it matter?

Fedor was seated on the bed in the darkness of the shuttered room. He had just switched off the flashlight, which he was holding in his gloved hand. The time was 4:50.

He had searched all four rooms, trying to envisage every possible hiding place, methodically examining each piece of furniture. At first, he had expected every minute to hear the door being flung open. Then, as his nerves calmed down, he had been able to concentrate on the job expeditiously and silently.

No sound came from within the building. Only the noise of an occasional passing car penetrated from the street below. Fedor was unconsciously sucking the small capsule, switching it from one side of his mouth to the other and rolling it up against his palate before restoring it to its original place under his tongue. The action was as mechanical as chewing a piece of gum: he no longer gave a thought to the contents.

Five to five. There was nothing to keep him there. Not a square inch remained unsearched. While he had concentrated on the job, his fear had evaporated, and when he had first sat down, he had been conscious only of his tiredness, the sort of heaviness following a dreary, unsatisfactory piece of work. But now he was becoming alert again, and he noticed that he was bathed in sweat. The central heating was still on, but this was not the cause of it. It was a deeper sweat that seemed to seep out of his bones, gluing his palms to the leather of his gloves.

He loosened his scarf, wondering why he was waiting till the 5:00 deadline, since there was nothing further to do. But in the back of his mind he knew the answer. He was afraid to leave. Far too experienced to indulge in pipe dreams, he had little hope of getting out as easily as he had got in. The temporary respite that he was enjoying merely meant that if a trap had been laid, it had not been laid by the police. They would have arrested him a moment after he had entered the apartment.

The probability was that one of the counterespionage services had taken over from them. They would let him complete his search, possibly because they did not know what he was searching for, and pick him up only when he had done their work for them. They could thus kill two birds with one stone. It was the usual form. No doubt, they were already waiting for him outside on the landing . . .

If only Pierre had provided him with a gun, he might have stood a chance, might have taken them by surprise and blasted his way out. But recently Pierre had developed an aversion for these tactics, as though he were afraid of hurting *them*. He seemed to imagine that by avoiding direct action, he might induce *them* to come to some sort of gentleman's agreement. He even seemed prepared to sacrifice his own agents to achieve it.

Pierre would no doubt have armed him if he had thought there was any chance of his retrieving the films. To protect the films, of course, not the agent—even his best one. But sizing up the situation as he had, Pierre had decided to remove the temptation, knowing that armed men were reluctant to kill themselves, but would rather fight to the bitter end, thus running the risk of being taken alive.

For Pierre had seemed certain that he would find nothing—had admitted as much. It had been an utterly useless mission, imposed by orders that should never have been followed blindly. But

Pierre would have stifled misgivings by telling himself that he was not gifted with divine sight, could not actually *know* that the films were not there. So, once again, he stood to lose a valuable man through his brand of caution.

Of course, once he himself was dead, Fedor reflected bitterly, it would never be known whether he had found anything or not. Pierre would merely report to Moscow, "Mission completed. Result negative. Operative dead," and that would be that.

Five o'clock. He could not remain there sitting on the bed forever. He got up and was racked by an uncontrollable spasm of anguish at the thought of the front door and what lay beyond it. He switched on his flashlight, switched it off again, and slowly groped his way out of the room. The capsule was now between two of his teeth: when the moment came, he only had to make his mind a blank and increase the pressure.

He jumped as a floorboard creaked. They would have heard it outside and known he was on his way. It was not fear of death or the few seconds' agony, as the poison cut through his body like a steel whip, that tormented him. It was the negation of life, the abrupt ending to all he had achieved and still hoped to achieve, that he would bring about by his own act, if not his own volition, gratuitously and futilely.

His outstretched fingers brushed against the

front door. He leaned forward, holding his breath, turned the lock, and slipped out on the landing. There was no one there. As he closed the door behind him, he let the air flow back into his lungs, experiencing a moment of sheer delight that he should still have an infinitesimal segment of life ahead of him. But, of course, they would be waiting outside the building, ready to hustle him into a car.

He lit his flashlight for a moment to locate the top of the staircase, then switched it off and started on his way down. He passed the concierge's lodge and reached the street. It appeared to be deserted. Nothing and no one moved under the white light of the lampposts. Turning left, he stepped out briskly with his hands in his pockets and his neck drawn down inside his coat collar, as though pierced by the cold. He knew that the apparent stillness must be deceptive and sensed the presence of someone behind him. It required all his self-control to prevent himself from glancing around and breaking into a run.

When he still found himself free after a quarter of a mile, he grasped what was going on. If "they" had not known what it was that he had been searching for in the apartment, they would have picked him up as soon as he left. Therefore, they must have found the microfilms themselves and be aware that his search had been fruitless. So now they would merely follow him, counting on him to lead them to his contact; hoping, eventually, to uncover every link in the chain.

For the first time since he had embarked on the mission, he felt a glimmer of hope: there might still be a chance to extricate himself. It would involve using all the old tricks to throw them off, with an additional factor to be taken into consideration. They would continue to follow him only for as long as they were confident that they had not been spotted. If he gave any sign that he had seen them, they would take him in charge at once.

Taking a small round mirror from his breast pocket, he clamped it to the crystal of his watch, then raised his wrist, without varying his pace, as though looking at the time. For little more than a second, he held the watch slightly above his shoulder, just long enough to catch sight of one of them slipping into the shadow of a doorway. The other man—there were sure to be two of them— would be lurking somewhere on the opposite sidewalk. They were about fifty yards behind him.

It was not going to be easy to lose them at this time of night, with empty streets, but they must be finding their own job equally tricky for the same reason.

He reached Trinité just as the Métro station opened, and was tempted to dive down into it. But he resisted, mindful that if he made things too difficult for them, they would bring the game to an abrupt end. And now that he was no longer a condemned man awaiting his executioners, he was beginning almost to enjoy it.

He became aware that the capsule was still in his mouth and remembered Pierre's final instructions: "Afterward, too, till you're certain you aren't being tailed." It looked as if Pierre had foreseen all along how things would turn out. It also looked, he thought wryly, as if Pierre had no great confidence in his ability to throw off his shadows.

Crossing the square, he branched off toward Saint-Lazare. He must give the impression of heading somewhere definite until he found the right moment to make his break. The town was beginning to stir. Cars passed more frequently, and the footsteps of an occasional pedestrian rang out on the asphalt. A sharp wind had sprung up, bringing down an acrid smell of soot from the chimneys.

He decided to wait another minute before taking a second brief glance in his mirror. Then it suddenly occurred to him that he had been behaving out of character ever since he left the apartment. A man in his situation *ought* to have looked around from time to time to make certain he was not being followed, whereas he had been acting as if the danger did not exist. It was not a mistake that he would have made if Pierre had not insisted on telling him the whole story. It had given him too much to think about, and in his confusion he had been a bit too clever. He should have relied on his natural impulses.

His lease of life depended on the psychology and experience of the men following him. Another small error of this kind could be enough to bring them down on him. It no longer seemed safe to use the watch trick again, but it was too late at this stage to start glancing behind him. For the moment, he would have to carry on blindly and try to find some other way to get a glimpse of them at well spaced-out intervals.

The vicinity of the station was like a small town of its own, isolated in the surrounding darkness, brightly lit, bustling, and noisy. The café opposite the main entrance was already open, and an elderly waiter was lugubriously polishing its windows. Trucks from the markets rumbled past, and a few bleary-eyed taxi drivers cruised around on the lookout for a last fare before going back to the garage.

Fedor went into the station. The concourse was crowded with departing passengers and the first wave of suburbanites surging off incoming trains. He took up a position under the clock, as though it were a prearranged meeting place, and kept his eyes on the entrances, concentrating on each new arrival. By memorizing as many details as possible, a profile, a hat, the color of a scarf, some prominent feature—anything that he would recognize if he saw it again—he hoped eventually to spot his shadows.

It was a game at which he was in a class by himself, aided by an exceptional visual memory developed and trained over the years. Yet even a keen observer would have failed to guess that he was playing it. To all outward appearance he was a man immersed in his own reflections, waiting patiently for someone to turn up, like the dozen or so others who waited beside him.

By the process of elimination, he had marked down the most stationary members of the crowd within a radius of fifty yards of him in a matter of minutes. Then, apparently growing restless, he took a short stroll up and down and returned to his former position. He had only instinct to guide him, but he thought he had identified one of them.

Presently he went through the motions of checking his watch with the clock, peered quite openly over the heads of the crowd, as though making one final search, and moved unhurriedly away. As he turned into the Cour de Rome, he saw with a mild feeling of satisfaction that his instinct had not let him down. The man whom he had spotted as his shadow, a youngish man, bareheaded, in a brown overcoat, was sauntering after him. He appeared to be on his own, but this did not mean anything. In this kind of shadowing, they frequently employed a system of relays. It was vital now to stay in character, to act like a man whose contact has failed to turn up at a rendezvous.

The first buses were drawn up outside the station. Fedor got into one bound for Montparnasse and sat down with his back to the rear platform. When he got off again at the end of the journey, without having looked around on the way, the man in the brown overcoat had disappeared. If he had ever been on the bus, he certainly was not on it now. Fedor went into a brasserie and ordered coffee, wondering whether he had not been mistaken after all, deceived by a mere coincidence. But as he left, he caught sight of a man loitering on the opposite sidewalk whom he recognized from two details memorized in the station: a buff briefcase tucked under one arm and a small, curly mustache.

By now, the town was fully awake. People were pouring into the gray morning from every aperture, merging into a solid stream and gliding slowly on their way. Fedor started walking up the boulevard waiting for his chance, with the uncomfortable knowledge that he could not afford to wait too long. If he continued to walk indefinitely, he would inevitably arouse suspicion. Had it been a routine police shadowing, when the shadows could be counted on not to pounce, there would have been nothing to worry about. He could have done pretty much as he liked, walked them off their feet, made a dash for it without any risk. But this was entirely different ...

His confidence began to seep away, and fear crept back. He was certain now that he was up against a well-trained team, with its whole organization and resources concentrated on one man: himself. He knew that he must do something "normal," but he could not think of anything to do. Out there in the street, after his wait at the station, the bus journey, and the brief interlude in the brasserie, there did not seem anywhere to go. All the familiar hideouts had to be avoided, and his aching muscles were calling out for rest. There seemed no way out but to invent a series of other rendezvous—rendezvous at which his contacts consistently failed to turn up—while he desperately sought an opportunity to throw his shadows off.

He pretended to look at his watch and quickened his pace. When he reached the Dôme, he went inside, sat down at a table, and ordered coffee and a rum. As he drank, he carefully kept the capsule under his tongue to avoid any risk of swallowing it. The man with the briefcase was no longer in sight, but there would be others outside, hemming him in. He stayed for half an hour, slumped on the banquette to get what rest he could, but watching everyone who came and went.

On leaving, he took the Boulevard Raspail and forked off down the Rue de Rennes to Saint-Germain. In the middle of a dense, slow-moving crowd, which he hoped might momentarily conceal him from his shadows and, in any case, must restrict their mobility, he decided that the moment had come. Knifing his way through with his shoulder, he made a sudden dart into the road and swung himself aboard the rear platform of a passing bus. There was no commotion behind him: it looked as if he had done it. The old tricks were always the best.

When the bus stopped at a red light, he waited for it to move on again and then slipped off. Now that he had burned his bridges, his only consideration was to put as much distance as possible between himself and his pursuers. Zigzagging through the traffic, he plunged down a side street and found himself outside Saint-Sulpice. A taxi was discharging its passengers just ahead of him. He jumped in and told the driver to take him to Ternes, then walked to the Parc Monceau.

Even now he was by no means certain that he had gotten away from them. He knew what a well-trained team, complete with relays, cars, and walkie-talkies, was capable of. Each man an expert, working on his own ground. He had never felt so utterly alone, abandoned inevitably by the network, with no one to call on for help. And for him it was enemy territory.

He went a short way into the park and turned around to come back again. As he did so, he

caught sight of the young man in the brown overcoat dawdling along despite the cold by the side
of a thin, dark woman with a scarf over her head.
And there would be more of them in the vicinity,
encircling him; more of them outside in cars, listening in on headphones, waiting to pick him up.

But nothing happened. He was allowed to continue on his way. It was even worse than it had
been in the bedroom of the apartment, when
danger had been concentrated in the two or three
men he had envisaged on the landing. Now the
whole town seemed to be closing in on him, but
with an almost casual, implacable leisureliness.
They were tiring him out, as an angler tires out a
hooked fish, by paying out the line. *What* could
they be waiting for?

It was possible that they had not yet realized
that he had spotted them. More probably, they imagined that he was now confident of having
thrown them off by his sudden dash. In either
case, they would still be hoping for him to lead
them to a contact. Apparently they did not rate
the danger of losing him very high.

He went on walking. It was getting close to
1:00, and he was beginning to feel hungry, but he
dared not go into a restaurant. He could not eat
without running the risk of swallowing the capsule, which seemed to have become part of his
tongue, growing out of it like a wart. For a moment he nursed the absurd idea that they knew it

was there and were patiently waiting for him to get rid of it so that they could take him alive.

He found himself eventually in the Rue Saint-Ferdinand near the Porte Maillot and went into a delicatessen to buy a ham roll. He could no longer see his shadows. They were certainly remarkably good at their job. When he came to a café, he locked himself into the rest room, sat down on the seat, and ate his roll, with the damp capsule balanced on the palm of his left hand.

Out in the street again, he caught sight of the dark woman in the scarf getting into a gray Dauphine. He plodded on. The entrance to a Métro station appeared on his right. He went down and boarded the first train that came along, not caring where it went. As he stood in the middle of the car, surrounded by impassive passengers preoccupied with newspapers or their private concerns, his sense of loneliness increased until it almost became a physical pain.

On a sudden impulse, he slipped out onto a platform just as the train doors were closing. In his state of apathy, he no longer hoped that this old trick would work. There were too many of *them*, and they seemed to know where he was going even when he did not know himself. They melted away, only to reappear ahead of him, apparently waiting confidently for him to turn up.

He had not bothered to look at the name of the

station, and had no idea where he was. In any case, what did it matter? As he trudged up a narrow, winding street, he recognized with resignation but no surprise the features of a man idling along on the opposite sidewalk. In the course of the next few hours, as he pursued his aimless journey, he counted more than ten familiar faces—unless he were going mad and suffering from hallucinations brought on by nervous fatigue.

As evening began to fall, he went from café to café, sitting down for a few minutes to drink a glass of wine before moving restlessly on. He was running short of money, and the temptation to call it a day recurred with increasing appeal each time he recollected, in sudden bursts of hatred and malice, that it lay within his power to end their game and nullify their hopes in a matter of seconds.

But he did not do it. He was prevented by an infinitesimal, tenacious fragment of hope of his own which he could not eradicate despite the inner knowledge that nothing could come of it, because even if he contrived to lose them by calling on the last dregs of his strength and cunning, he could never return home or contact the network again. There would never be any certainty that he had finally gotten rid of them, and in those circumstances he could not run the risk of leading them to Pierre. He could see nothing ahead of him but, at best, a friendless nomadic existence, made even more insupportable by the contant fear of being recognized. Yet something still stopped him from throwing his hand in before he must.

His utter exhaustion dictated his next move. He went into a small, shabby hotel and booked a room. His lack of luggage prompted the manageress to demand payment in advance, and it was with a sense of immense relief that he found he still had just enough money to satisfy it. To his jaundiced eye, she resembled the thin, dark woman, grown twenty years older.

Upstairs in the bedroom, a glance from the window confirmed what he had already foreseen. *They* were there—two strangers, looking up from the opposite sidewalk without any attempt at concealment, as though it no longer mattered whether he caught sight of them or not. Once again, he wondered what they could be waiting for.

He had kept on his coat and scarf, for it was cold in the dismal room, which smelled musty and damp. The iron bedstead was covered with a thin once-white cotton bedspread. The red tiles on the floor were loose and uneven. Motionless, his forehead pressed against the glass, he stared down at them, while they continued to stare back, their heads in the air. In a sudden fit of childishness, he blew a thin coat of vapor over the pane, then rubbed a small circle in the center of it, through which he could still look out. Presently they were joined by a third man with a long, deeply lined face. After a brief conversation, he stared up, too. Then he appeared to issue orders, for the two men nodded and started across the road.

Fedor moved away from the window and lay down on the bed, resting the back of his head on his crossed hands. The wait seemed endless before he heard footsteps on the stairs and idly wondered whether there would be two of them or all three. He wondered, too, exactly what was going on in their minds at this particular moment. Now that the game had reached its final stage, he felt completely detached, as though he were no longer involved in it.

Someone cleared his throat outside in the corridor. Then there was a gentle knock on the door, almost the knock of a friend. Without moving, Fedor called, "Come in!" His only feeling was one of mild curiosity. What on earth were they up to? The door opened and they came in, one behind the other. The first man had his hand in the pocket of his raincoat: the barrel of his gun was almost visible.

"Now, how about a little talk, my friend?" he said breezily. "It shouldn't be difficult to come to some sort of agreement."

Fedor smiled without answering. Out of the corner of his eye, he was watching the second man advancing gingerly, as though he were entering a sickroom. There were just the two of them. He had bet on there being two, and even at this moment he derived some slight satisfaction from having guessed right.

The first man picked up a chair and turned it toward the bed without taking his eyes off Fedor or releasing his hold on the revolver. But these were only routine precautions. They were about to get down to business and undoubtedly would come to terms.

Fedor burst the capsule with a snap of his teeth. The plastic covering was much softer than he had expected . . .

When one of the two men opened the window to beckon to him, Coster knew at once what must have happened. He had been afraid of it ever since the chase had gotten under way. He climbed the stairs to the bedroom, where Fedor's body lay twisted on the bed. The man with the breezy manner had already begun to search it. He produced nothing beyond a few loose coins, a flashlight, and a small tool kit, containing skeleton keys.

Coster studied the dead man's face. He could not recollect ever having seen it before. And there would certainly be nothing on him by which he could be identified. They would have to follow the same procedure as the police had employed with Krestowicz. A headline in the papers—"Unknown Man Found Dead in Hotel Bedroom"—and a photograph to go with it. This time, though, the police surgeon and the undertaker would have more difficulty in making the face photogenic: strychnine produced a rictus that was hard to eliminate. But someone, a neighbor or a cleaning woman, would probably recognize him, and one of his covers would be blown. And short of an unlikely stroke of luck, that would be as far as they would get.

The two men started on the job of stripping the body. Coster watched them with the same feeling of distaste that he would have experienced in watching a pack of hounds leaping on their dead quarry. But it had to be done. Better not to start wondering just how much the victim had suffered during the desperate flight that had finally come to an end in this sordid, fourth-rate hotel.

It would be more constructive to dig up a word of praise for those involved in the chase. They had done well to bring off this first experiment in applying a new technique to shadowing; shadowing "by circles," whereby an area within a radius of 150 yards was completely sealed off, and it was only necessary to employ one tail at a time. If the "subject" succeeded in throwing him off, he would be picked up again by someone else when he reached the circumference of the circle. The circle or circles were extremely mobile and could be re-formed as and where required. It was an operation demanding a large number of trained men and a large amount of equipment, which made it too expensive for use on everyday police shadowings. It was a "reserve weapon" for special occasions.

One of the two men looked up after ripping

open the linings of the dead man's clothes. "Nothing there. Goes without saying."

Coster scratched his bristly chin. He had not had time to shave since the previous morning—like the man on the bed.

"Yes, it goes without saying," he agreed absentmindedly.

The naked body was that of a well-built man, some years short of middle age. There was a damp stain on the coverlet between his thighs, and the pungent smell of urine drifted through the room.

The two men, looking slightly crestfallen, stood around, waiting for orders.

"You couldn't have prevented it," Coster said without expression.

"I'll swear he never moved a finger. We kept our eyes on him the whole time."

Coster shrugged. "He must have had whatever it was in his mouth. It can't be helped. You did a good job, just the same."

The operation had been successful. But alas, the patient had died . . .

NINE

That morning, Dominique awoke at 5:00 to the slow realization that she was alone in the fishing boat. She could only imagine that Maria and Tom had gone off on another hunt for the *Andromeda,* leaving her to sleep it out, and would be back. But stiff and cold, she decided to stretch her legs and try to join them. It was still dark as she jumped down onto the quay, and the flickering lights from the harbor's scattered lampposts scarcely penetrated it.

There was no one in sight as she left the fishermen's section of the port and made her way to the jetty where the big yachts were moored. She paused from time to time to cup her hands into a megaphone and call out Maria's name, but meeting with no response, she finally went back to the boat and continued to call from there.

Then she suddenly remembered the loss of the revolver and plunged her hand into her coat pocket. The money was still there. Perhaps they had gone into town or just for a walk to get warm. But she still clung to the hope that they had found the *Andromeda* somewhere where she had failed to look and would be back any minute to confirm that their friend had room aboard for her, too. Without any thought for the past or the future, all she wanted was to be with them again; not to be left alone in this deserted, windswept harbor.

Afraid to leave the boat again in case she missed them when they returned, she planted herself firmly in front of it, legs apart, and waited. She should never have left it in the first place. They might well have come back while she was away looking for them on the jetty, in which case they would not be looking for her, all three of them involved in a ridiculous game of hide-and-seek. She felt a wave of affection for Maria, with whom she had scarcely exchanged a dozen words, as she recollected the childish, innocent face and the swollen stomach, which somehow suggested a little girl who had stuffed a cushion into her skirt for fun rather than an actual pregnancy.

Presently it occurred to her that if they had found the yacht, they might be waiting on board till daylight before coming to wake her; in which case, she could save them a journey. She set off again, peering at the names of the various boats, just visible in the first pale glimmer of dawn, as the three of them had done when they first arrived. A man with his hands in his pockets and a woolen cap pulled down over his eyebrows suddenly appeared on the deck of a yacht alongside her. As soon as he caught sight of her, he whistled and beckoned to her to come aboard. She gave him a startled glance and hurried on, pursued by his raucous laughter.

Forgetting her original objective in her anxiety to get away from him, she passed through an archway and found herself in the old town—narrow streets running uphill from a marketplace, where men were setting up trestle stalls. She walked up one of the streets till she came to the shopping center and bought a croissant and a copy of *Nice-matin*, which she read on the sidewalk as she ate. Kola's photograph appeared on the third page with a name underneath it: "Nicolas Balsier, insurance agent."

Her eyes slid blankly from the familiar face to the unknown name before passing on to the photograph of Françoise Oscarsen alongside them. The accompanying news story was short and made no reference to herself. It gave a vague two-line description of the woman seen running away from the apartment, which bore little resemblance to her appearance then and none to her present one.

She muttered, "It's not possible . . . !" and looked around her in a daze, half expecting for a fraction of a second to wake up in her bedroom in the Avenue Mozart after a terrifyingly realistic nightmare. Then, pulling herself together, she slowly read through the article again. As she finished it, her eye was caught by a headline in the stop-press: "Mysterious Death of Françoise Oscarsen in Lariboisière Hospital. Unknown Woman Responsible?"

She grasped that Kola must have been leading a double life, passing under the name of Balsier in the Rue Clauzel, but no effort of her imagination could take her beyond this. The murder of the woman in the hospital brought nothing but a dim recollection; a recollection somehow connected with Kola's furious, scarcely recognizable face as he had twisted her wrists . . .

She slipped the paper into her pocket and continued on her way. With the sun out, the weather had become almost mild. She knew nothing of the south of France except for what she had seen of it in movies. As a child she had spent all her summer holidays in Brittany, and Kola had loathed the sea. The memory of those last three years, married to him, broke up and floated away like fragments of ragged cloud. Here in the sunshine they seemed as far away and unreal as the snow she had encountered on the way down. The whole thing had been a sham and an illusion from the beginning.

Catching sight of a pharmacy, she went inside and bought a bottle of Oréal and a package of razor blades, then set out in search of the public baths. She had no means of knowing that by now every Soviet network in Europe had received a detailed description of her and was in the process of implementing the instructions accompanying it. It was just one item among many—though its classification under "Security" gave it top priority—that had been meshed into the machine that morning; a machine that operated with all the precision of a computer.

When she found the baths, Dominique locked herself into one of the cabins and cut her hair short with a razor blade in much the same way as she had done it during her time at the Beaux-Arts. She then applied the bleach and had a bath. It made her drowsy, and she woke herself up with cold water before giving herself a shampoo and getting dressed again. When she looked in the mirror, the reflection might have been that of herself at nineteen. The blond hair, cut all anyhow, with a strand coming down over her forehead, made her face rounder and younger. She turned away from it with a pang of nostalgia and concentrated on the present.

She carefully picked up all the loose tresses from the floor, braided them, and stuffed them in her pocket; then, noticing her wedding ring, she took it off and slipped it in with the hair. A corner of the wet towel served to remove most of the mud and dust from her raincoat and boots. When she was outside again, she headed back to the harbor more from an instinctive desire to return to a familiar place than for any set purpose. She no longer expected to meet up with Maria and Tom again, and no longer wanted to. Her changed appearance would call for a plausible explanation which, for the moment, she was incapable of inventing.

The harbor was beginning to show signs of life. There were muted sounds of hammering from somewhere in the distance. A man was scraping a keel and another sluicing down a deck. Two or three idlers, their caps on the back of their heads, were lounging about the quays. The wind had almost died away, but a light swell still splashed up against the stonework, making the masts sway in rhythm. There was no sign of the *Andromeda*.

Dominique wandered through a narrow archway under the jetty and came on a pebbled beach at the foot of the old ramparts. Scores of screeching, predatory sea gulls were swooping down into the troughs of the waves and zooming up again. She climbed to the grassy terrace on top of the ramparts, overlooking the projecting rocks, and discovered a small bay. A large schooner was anchored in the middle of it. All alone, with flaking paint, deserted decks, and towering masts, she looked as if she had been abandoned after a long voyage, but she was rocking up and down in the swell with lofty unconcern. Dominique sat down on the grass, staring at the ship, with her chin supported on her fists.

"If you like the look of her, I'll sell her to you."

She had not heard the man approach and jerked around, startled, to find him within a few feet of her. Tall and shaggy, with a wide, bushy beard, he was wearing faded jeans, a seaman's jacket with all the buttons missing, and dirty rope-soled sandals.

"Is she yours?"

"No, but I can sell her for the owner." His cheeks crinkled up in a smile. "What would you do with her if you bought her?"

The smile warmed her, and she said jauntily, "Live in her, of course."

"With lace curtains over the portholes and creepers growing up the mast?"

"No, she's lovely as she is," Dominique answered, adding as an afterthought, "But I'd give her a coat of paint."

He scratched his cheek and frowned with one eyebrow as though what she had just said merited serious consideration, then squatted down beside her with his buttocks resting on his heels. She would have found it difficult to make a guess at his age. There was an alertness and penetration in his eyes that seemed to belie the wrinkles and gray hair.

"She isn't the *Andromeda*, by any chance?" she asked.

"No. Got your constellations wrong. She's the *Vega*. Clyde-built in 1904. You won't easily find another old lady of sixty-seven with her looks! She's had a full life, too. Been in the Pacific and the China seas, won a race or two, and there's some talk of her having done a bit of smuggling in her time."

"And now ... ?"

"Now she's reduced to living with a caretaker. Me. Sad, but there it is ...."

"Stuck there till her dying days?"

The man shrugged. "She's as well off there as anywhere else. As long as she isn't bought by some nightclub pimp and turned into a brothel." After a pause, he asked, "Were you looking for the *Andromeda?*"

"Not especially," Dominique said cautiously. "A friend of mine happened to mention that she was in Antibes, that's all."

"She was, but she sailed for Spain two weeks ago." He gestured toward the *Vega*. "If you're interested in sailing ships, how about having some lunch with me? I can offer you oysters and sea urchins. Only red wine to go with them, though."

"I don't think I will, but thanks all the same."

"Maybe some other time ..." he said placidly,

and stood up, scratching at a paint stain on his jacket. Before strolling off, he took an old pipe with a curved stem out of his pocket and stuck it in his mouth without filling it.

Dominique stayed on where she was, contemplating the schooner and mildly regretting her refusal; it had been prompted by her recollection of the man who had whistled at her earlier that morning. But suddenly thinking of the problems that lay ahead if, by some extraordinary piece of luck, she remained at liberty, she realized that she was in no position to indulge in such reactions.

After a time, she saw a dinghy put out from the shore, bobbing up and down like a cork. Pipe in mouth, the man was standing up in her, propelling her along with one oar, heading toward his ship on his own.

When he had reached Nice about 11:00 on the previous evening, the truck driver had garaged his vehicle and gone straight off to get some sleep, utterly exhausted. Twenty-four hours on the road took it out of you when you were no longer in the first flush of youth.

He had slept till 9:00, eaten a large breakfast, and then returned to the garage to unload the cargo. He had no reason to hurry since he was his own boss. With business none too good, he was always glad to pick up a few francs on the side by giving people a lift, as he had done on the previous

night. Boys or girls, it was all one to him as long as
they could afford to pay.

The boy who should have been there to help
him had not turned up yet, so he undid the back
flap of the truck himself and climbed in. As he
edged forward, the toe of his shoe came up against
the revolver. He had found some odd things before, but never this. What made it even more surprising was that it should be just where the girls
had been lying all through the trip. Of course, girls
nowadays . . . !

A cold shudder ran up his spine as he thought of
what might have happened to him during the
night if . . . Then, hearing his assistant approaching, he picked up the gun and slipped it into his
pocket. It monopolized his mind all through the
unloading and went some way toward spoiling his
appetite for lunch. Admittedly, nothing *had* happened, so it was senseless to get worked up about
it, but he read the papers and listened to the radio
and even knew one or two drivers, personally, who
had been held up on the road. And there was no
getting away from it—boys and girls did not carry
revolvers just for the fun of it. If they had not
made use of it during the journey, it could only be
because no suitable opportunity had presented itself. He still had a clear mental picture of them;
even of the two girls, whom he had had time to get
a good look at during the stop at the café. Nevertheless he was reluctant to go to the police. In his

experience, you never got a word of thanks and often ended up, metaphorically, with a kick in the ass.

But 3:00 saw him in the police station, partly because he could not think of any other way to spend the afternoon—he was not due to start on his return trip till the following day. Partly, too, because he had no idea what to do with the gun. Nothing would have induced him to keep it. There were two bullets missing.

The sergeant took down his statement, relieved him of the revolver, handling it gingerly by the barrel, and made the inevitable corny joke: "If it isn't claimed within a year . . ." Then he sniffed it, and his eyebrows rose. He reached for the telephone.

Two minutes later, the driver was entering the superintendent's office accompanied by the sergeant carrying the revolver in a duster. The superintendent took a quick look at the gun, then listened while the driver repeated his statement. In common with police all over the country, he had received a priority "Wanted" message, giving the description of a woman suspected of murder in Paris; a murder committed with a 7.65 mm. caliber firearm. The driver's description of one of the two women to whom he had given a lift tallied with it exactly.

The superintendent pushed the message aside and looked up. "You say the young man was with you in the cab all through the trip. Did he talk to you?"

The driver eyed him pityingly. "Of course, he did. It stands to reason. He wouldn't keep his trap shut for twenty-four hours, would he?"

Unruffled, the superintendent asked, "Did he say anything about the two girls with him?"

"No, never mentioned 'em. The one, who was expecting, seemed to be his wife . . . Well, more or less; you never know nowadays . . . I suppose she could have been his sister, for that matter: he didn't say. When he wasn't asleep, he talked mostly about all the different countries he'd been to. Struck me he was putting it on a bit, considering his age."

"How about the other girl? Did he seem to know her well?"

"He seemed to know 'em both about the same. Difficult to tell, though: neither girl talked much."

"Where were they going to in Antibes? Did they happen to mention it?"

"No." The driver scowled. All these damn fool questions! He knew he shouldn't have come. Then he remembered something. "Wait a minute! They didn't mention it in so many words, but they did ask me the way to the harbor when I dropped them off, if that's any help."

The superintendent nodded to the sergeant, who took the driver out, made him read and sign his statement, checked his papers, and wrote down his address. The driver became increasingly surly, and by the time he left, he was in one hell of a temper. Catch him doing his duty again!

The instructions that the superintendent had received along with the woman's description were clear enough.

(*a*) He was to report to Paris immediately if she was sighted.

(*b*) He was not to arrest her.

They made no sense to him, but he supposed that the powers-that-be in Paris knew what they were up to.

It seemed a pity, all the same. The harbor at Antibes was comparatively small, and a group of three, two of them easily recognizable, would be easy enough to spot. Given a free hand, he would have had them under lock and key by nightfall.

He sighed resignedly and dialed the P.J.'s number in Paris.

||||||||||||||||||||||||||||||||||||||||||||||||||||||||||||||||||||||||||||||||||||||||||||||||||||||||||||||||||||||||||||||||||||||||||

TEN

At 8:00 in the evening of the same day, January 22, Coster took a last look at the dead man on the bed and went downstairs to see the manageress, leaving his two subordinates to deal with the formalities, notify the police, and arrange for the body to be taken to the Medical-Legal Institute. Later, they would have to release the news of the unknown man's suicide to the press and provide them with photographs for publication on the following morning.

Pierre was in his apartment, running through

the late editions of the evening papers. At 3:30 that morning, the time when Fedor was due to make his entry into the Rue Clauzel apartment, he had begun his inconspicuous vigil behind a clump of bushes in the Avenue Foch, some fifty yards from the litter basket. At 6:30 he had given up and gone home. Fedor had had an hour and a half to reach the rendezvous and would not be coming now . . . or ever.

Since reaching his apartment, he had been listening to radio news bulletins and combing the papers for confirmation of his assumption that his agent was dead, sustaining himself by drinking endless cups of tea and nibbling at lumps of sugar. Though, so far, the Paris papers contained nothing that could be related to Fedor, they did report that Balsier had been identified as Krestowicz by his cleaning woman and an employee at his shop. The police were anxious to interview his wife, who had disappeared in "mysterious circumstances" and was thought likely to be able to assist them in their inquiries. A photograph of Dominique Krestowicz, none too well reproduced, headed the column.

To all appearances, the police were still in charge of the case and saw nothing more in it than a run-of-the-mill domestic crime, triggered off by jealousy. In concentrating their suspicion on Kola's wife, they obviously shared the same conclusion to which Pierre had come two days before, and there was a quirk of satisfaction on his face as he went to put the kettle on for the eighth time.

An additional source of satisfaction lay in the message that he had received an hour earlier. The two torpedoes sent from Moscow were due to arrive on the following morning.

While Pierre was thinking of them in the abstract, as important pieces in a complicated game, one of the two torpedoes—cover name "Tancred" —was waiting in the airport bar at Stockholm for his Paris flight to be called. All departures had been held up for eighteen hours by bad weather. He had set out the night before, traveling by air to Finland and then by boat to Sweden. A man of infinite patience, he was unconcerned at the delay and still hoped to reach Paris in time to get a good night's sleep before meeting his contact.

He had no idea what this new mission involved and was in no particular hurry to find out. A glass of excellent beer in his hand, he was idly watching the snow drift down outside and looking forward to a bed with well-laundered sheets in a good hotel. After that, he would be operating on his own, largely by instinct, like an expert skier on a downhill run.

He enjoyed traveling, and his chosen profession provided him with frequent opportunities to indulge in it. That was one of its great advantages.

The second torpedo—cover name "Viktor"—had followed a different route, crossing Germany by train. At this moment, he was lying in a drawer at the Stuttgart morgue. With two hours between trains, he had made a sortie from the station in search of a restaurant serving his favorite sausages. Knocked down by a car, he had suffered a broken spine and a fractured skull. It had all happened very quickly, the car had not stopped, and the few passersby had seen little of the occurrence owing to the prevailing fog.

It had probably been a genuine accident, but when this kind of thing happened to torpedoes, there was always a shadow of doubt. Like people leaving a trail of debts behind them wherever they went, they always ran the risk of being unexpectedly recognized. And the more they traveled, the more debts they incurred. That was one of the profession's disadvantages.

At 8:05, after giving the manageress a few succinct explanations, Coster went back to his car to send an "operation completed" message to the rest of his team. His driver told him that headquarters had been trying to get in touch with him since 5:00, which led to his learning that Dominique Krestowicz had probably been located in the vicinity of Antibes and that, equally probably, the weapon used in the Rue Clauzel had come to light.

In addition, the two agents, sent that morning to

make inquiries at the LICOM factory at Lyon, had reported that one of the directors' secretaries, Sylvia Barsouin, had failed to turn up for work for several days without furnishing any explanation. The personnel branch had tried to get in touch with her at her home address without success. Sylvia Barsouin had had access to the office in which the photographed documents were kept.

Seated on a corner of his desk, Coster dictated a press release: "Dominique Krestowicz, sought in connection with the murder of her husband, antique dealer Nicolas Krestowicz, is reported seen at Antibes. The police are pursuing their inquiries." Then he picked up the telephone and rang Orly to find out the departure times of planes to Nice. He had decided to go there on his own. From now on, everything would have to be handled with kid gloves.

As he had expected, little had come of his painstaking search of the Krestowiczes' apartment the evening before. It had yielded nothing as far as the antique dealer was concerned; at least, nothing compromising. But from her personal possessions and a number of photograph albums, he had been able to form some sort of impression of the wife; a vague idea of how her mind might work . . .

At 9:00, Maria and Tom were dining on bread and salami on one of the small beaches at Cadaqués. It was Tom who had decided to leave at

4:00 that morning. Since the *Andromeda* was no longer at Antibes, he knew it must be at Alicante at this time of year. They had not awakened Dominique to tell her their plans in case she insisted on coming, too. Hitchhiking for three just did not work. They had stationed themselves at the entrance to the autoroute and had the good luck to be picked up by a truck going straight to Sète. As dusk fell, they had crossed into Spain.

Dominique was wondering where she was going to spend the night. That afternoon, she had gone for a walk away from the town along the edge of the sea, looking for somewhere to have a nap. At Cap d'Antibes, she had turned off up a narrow path, which had eventually brought her to the lighthouse. Behind it, she had found a sheltered copse where she had stretched out in the sun and promptly fallen asleep.

She had been awakened by the persistent braying of a donkey anxious to be taken to its stable. The sun was setting, and the air was cold again. She went up to the donkey to pat its muzzle, but it jerked its head away contemptuously. As she set off down the hill, she reflected with a flicker of amusement that she had not been very successful lately in her social contacts. But her sleep had done her good; she was a resilient woman, mentally and physically, recovering as swiftly as she had collapsed.

The outlook was certainly far from bright, and in her present predicament there was little she could do to improve it; she could only take things as they came and try not to get upset. The immediate, basic problem to be faced was that of existence—everything else was secondary to that. Somehow or other she must manage to keep going on the small resources left her until something turned up . . .

She wandered back to the small beach behind the jetty that she had discovered that morning, smoothed out a flat place for herself among the pebbles, and sat down. On the way she had bought a pack of Gauloises, some sandwiches, and a Paris paper. The paper carried the news that Kola had been identified under his correct name but seemed no better informed on the details of his double life than she was. Reading between the lines, she gathered, without any particular emotion, that she was the chief—in fact, the only—suspect. Her photograph at the top of the column, she decided, was unlikely to be recognized by anyone but herself.

The police must have already searched the apartment to dig it out of the drawer where she had tucked it away. It was a studio portrait, taken two years before at Kola's insistence, and it made her look almost absurdly sophisticated. She had never liked it, and she could not imagine why the police had chosen it in preference to a snapshot from one of the albums, which would have shown her as she really was. Still, in the circumstances, she was grateful.

The description of her beneath the photograph was accurate enough as far as it went and must have been supplied by Percy or the cleaning woman. It did not, however, extend to her clothes, though it made a guess, no doubt based on the fact that it had been raining when she left: "Probably wearing a raincoat and boots." All in all, it did not seem to present much of a threat.

She did not have her identity card on her, since she only carried it when traveling, and for a moment this worried her; then she realized that she could scarcely have risked producing it in any case. Money was a more serious matter: after paying the truck driver and making her few small purchases, she had only 140 francs left. It no longer seemed a small fortune. After eating the sandwiches, she lit a cigarette and stared out at the dim shape of the *Vega*, rocking gently in the bay. There was no sign of life on board; not even a riding light.

Thinking back to the column in the newspaper, with its euphemistic reference to "helping the police with their inquiries," she supposed that the sensible thing to do would be to place herself in the hands of a lawyer and hope that he might secure her acquittal on the grounds of extenuating circumstances. But she had no intention of doing it. She could face the possibility, even the probability, of being found by the police in the end, but tamely to give herself up was out of the question.

Meanwhile, she wondered where she was going to spend the night. She did not relish the prospect of returning to the fishing boat, which would be cold and lonely without Maria and Tom, but unable to conjure up an alternative, she finally resigned herself to it. Throwing away her cigarette, she stood up. As she turned to leave, she could just make out a dim figure which had not been there when she arrived, sitting on a bench at the foot of the ramparts. Her way back to the arch in the jetty took her past it, and she recognized the man from the *Vega*, lounging with his legs stretched out in front of him, sucking at his empty pipe.

He said good evening, and she stopped, wondering whether he had followed her onto the beach or always took a breath of air there in the evenings. When he patted the vacant half of the bench with the palm of his hand, she sat down beside him, largely because he was the only human being with whom she had made some sort of contact during the day. But she did it tentatively, like a cat sniffing around before deciding to stay.

Without turning his head or removing his pipe, he said slowly, "None of my business and I don't want to butt in, but you look as if you were going through a rough time. If I'm right and you're stuck for somewhere to sleep, you're welcome to the *Vega* for the night. I can easily find somewhere else to sleep."

The unexpected kindness after her desolate day brought her to the verge of tears. She wanted to jump at the offer, but a recently developed wariness made her hesitate. It was not his motives that she mistrusted but his friendliness: she saw it leading to a series of tactful questions, a big-brotherly invitation to confide in him, which would be difficult to ward off.

As if he guessed what was worrying her, he added, "There's one condition, though. Don't expect me to listen to the story of your life. I've had about as many sad stories as I can take." He gave a sudden snort of laughter. "No reflection on your sex. Most of 'em came from men."

She smiled with relief. "I'll spare you . . . I promise!"

He rowed her out in the dinghy. Standing on the *Vega*'s broad deck, with the masts, thick as tree trunks, towering above her, the schooner seemed even larger than she had expected. The man hovered beside her with the anxiety of a child anxious to elicit admiration for a treasured possession.

"Just imagine the size of crew needed to handle her!"

He bustled her off on a tour of the deck, stepping

145

over rusty chains, skirting shattered skylights and coils of rotting rope. The bright moonlight produced furtive, strange-shaped shadows, which glided to and fro with the motion of the boat.

He muttered half-apologetically, "Can't keep her up on my own. It'd take me a month of Sundays just to holystone the decks," and led her aft to show off the huge wheel, which came up to her chin. On the way, he volunteered the information that his name was Jean but did not appear to expect her to reciprocate, for he went on without a pause. "Looks as if the weather's changing. I shouldn't be surprised if we got an east wind."

Stooping to open a small door in the deckhouse, he jumped down inside and lit an oil lamp; then, beckoning to her to follow, opened another door on the far side to disclose a large cabin with two wide bunks fixed to opposite walls.

"Here's where you'll sleep. There's a bathroom at the back. Afraid the bath doesn't work, but the sink and toilet are okay. Hungry?"

Dominique shook her head. A dirty eiderdown half-covered rumpled sheets on one of the bunks. Pipes, cigarette butts, and old newspapers lay scattered around. The photograph of a big, long-haired mongrel was nailed to one of the bulwarks.

"That's my dog, Sando. Had to have him put away last year."

She made vague murmurs of sympathy, though

his matter-of-fact tone of voice had not invited any. The cabin was stuffy and smelled of tobacco, and the roll was more perceptible in it than up on deck, but it was much as she had pictured it and gave her the sense of security for which she had hoped—a feeling of being snugly tucked away beyond anyone's reach.

Nevertheless, she felt compelled to protest. "I can't take your cabin! There must be lots of others. I don't mind where I sleep."

He ran a hand through his beard, smiling. "I'll show you the others in the morning, but you'd better stay here for tonight. They're not in too good shape." He seemed to be enjoying a private joke of his own.

"But where'll you sleep?"

"I'll find somewhere ashore, like I told you. You'll have the *Vega* to yourself."

"I can't turn you out! Let me sleep in that little hut place." She looked at him, distressed, then sat down wearily on the unmade bunk. "This is too ridiculous! You sleep in your bunk, and I'll take this one. Why on earth not?"

He laughed and shook his head. "Because you wouldn't sleep a wink with me here. Or you'd have nightmares." He moved over to a cupboard, took out sheets, blankets, and a bolster, and tossed them down beside her. Then, setting the lamp down on a table, he bundled up his own bedclothes and mattress. "Let's cut out all this damn politeness before we both go crazy. I'll sleep on deck. I'm quite used to it. Now, get to bed and stop fussing! Good night!"

He turned around in the doorway. "There's a bolt on your side. Close it tight. It isn't necessary, but you'll feel a whole lot safer . . ."

ELEVEN

Pierre read the news of the "unknown man's" death in next morning's papers and recognized Fedor in the accompanying photographs. He had been found in a hotel bedroom at 7:30 on the previous evening without any identity papers on him, and foul play was not suspected. There were no further details.

But to Pierre, it was clear enough that Fedor had been tailed as soon as he left the apartment and had finally abandoned any hope of shaking off his shadows. Shadowing as efficient as that could only have been carried out by one of the counterespionage services, and their involvement must mean that the microfilms had somehow fallen into their hands. There was no longer any doubt as to how things stood.

With three deaths in three days, the network was beginning to disintegrate. But, worse still, counterespionage now had three separate bases from which to launch their inquiries, each of them a potential danger, since the dead could sometimes be made to yield information by skilled investigators. Despite all the precautions, there was no certainty that meticulous searching into the pasts of Krestowicz, Oscarsen, and Fedor, who would soon be identified, would not eventually turn up a thread leading to Pierre.

And there was a fourth source of danger in Dominique Krestowicz, whose knowledge of the network's setup was impossible to assess. But there was a stroke of luck in her case, for which he had not dared to hope. Another part of the newspaper carried a report of her having been sighted at Antibes. It did not specify by whom, but it could not have been the police, or they would certainly have picked her up. So there still remained a chance of getting to her first.

Pierre folded the paper and put it in his pocket. It was time to keep his separate rendezvous with the two torpedoes.

At 9:30, inconspicuous in the crowded Etoile Métro station, Tancred was leaning against the wall to the right of the newsstand, recognizable by his pipe, the copy of *Le Monde* tucked under his arm and the open *Paris Match*, in which he appeared to be engrossed.

Pierre approached him, holding out his hand. "Not making a mistake, am I? You are the new accountant?"

Tancred shook the hand and gave him a cool smile. "That's right. The temporary one. Have we time for a cup of coffee?"

He was a young man in a dark, well-cut suit, bought in Spain on one of his other missions, with deep-blue eyes and an innocent, friendly expression. Though he seemed completely relaxed, he was carefully checking each word of the recognition phrases.

Pierre looked at his watch. "Yes, just time, if we hurry. I've had breakfast already."

He liked what he saw of the other man, undeceived by the surface amiability. He sensed the ruthless efficiency that lay beneath it. As soon as they were outside walking down the Champs-Elysées, he briefed him on the mission ahead of him in a few curt sentences.

"The woman's just been sighted in Antibes," he said in conclusion, and handed him the newspaper. "I'll let you have a better photograph of her later."

Tancred studied the photograph for a moment, then read the paragraph below it.

"If she's seen this, she won't still be there," he said slowly.

It was a reasonable assumption, but Pierre had already rejected it. "That's what everyone's liable to think, including the police and counterespionage. But she's an intelligent woman. If the papers reported me to be somewhere or other, I'd damn well stay there, counting on it being the last place anyone would bother to look. And my guess is that she'll have done the same."

Tancred smiled. "There's nothing to stop the others from guessing that, too."

Pierre had worked with torpedoes before and knew that they had acquired a privileged status which gave them the right to argue and discuss their missions far more freely than regular agents. He did not approve, but he accepted.

"It's possible," he admitted, "but I don't think it's likely. I've got a slight edge on them. I know she's capable of that sort of reasoning, and they don't." After a pause, he added sharply, "In any case, we've no choice. If we don't look for her in Antibes, where the hell do we look?"

"It hasn't occurred to you that it may be a trap?"

The lines around Pierre's mouth tightened. He did not appreciate being taught his own job. He said coldly, "I haven't reached the age of fifty-two by overlooking possibilities, remote or otherwise."

Tancred accepted the snub, unruffled. He seemed

about to ask a further question, but Pierre forestalled him. "Naturally, I'll get an okay from Control later in the day, but I'll be surprised if they don't agree. I've reserved a room for you at the Hôtel des Acacias. Do you know Paris?"

"Up to a point. I've never been here before, but I went through the usual briefing."

"What's your cover?"

"Selki. Finnish nationality. Cameraman."

Tancred was well aware that the other man already knew these details and was mildly amused that he should still go in for such old-fashioned, sudden security checks. Nevertheless, he found him likable—a fussy, aging war horse, fast approaching the time when he would be put out to pasture.

"Meet me outside the Passy Métro at nineteen fifteen hours," Pierre went on. "And have your equipment ready. You'll contact your friend when you get to Antibes."

Tancred resisted an impulse to click his heels and salute as Pierre melted away into the crowd. He was sorry that Pierre had not brought the better photograph with him. He would have liked to study it at leisure, stretched out on the bed in his hotel room. It was an important part of his technique, particularly when the target was a woman. By studying their photographs in this way, he developed a curious rapport with his "subjects," which finally enabled him to predict their thought processes and reactions with an accuracy that bordered on the miraculous.

He decided to spend the rest of the morning on a sight-seeing tour of Paris, which he only knew from street maps and models. There would be ample time in the afternoon to pick up the necessary equipment from the store—a store, catering exclusively to members of his profession, of which even resident-agents and heads of networks remained in ignorance.

Pierre waited in vain at the Palais-Royal for Viktor, the second torpedo, due to meet him there at 10:30. At 10:35 he left. It was always dangerous to wait at a rendezvous for more than a few minutes when a contact failed to turn up on time, and particularly so in the present circumstances.

He went back to his apartment, tense and uneasy. As usual, a second rendezvous had been prearranged—the Louvre Métro at 1:00—in case some casual mishap should prevent either party from keeping the first one. He decided to await the outcome before reporting to Moscow and asking for final instructions. The situation, quite apart from the missing torpedo, would justify him in sending an urgent message outside the regular transmission hours.

Coster had arrived in Nice on a night flight. At 9:30 on this same morning, January 23, he was closeted with the police superintendent. The latter was impressed by Special Services' intervention in the affair and was doing his best to be helpful, though unhappily aware that he had not much to contribute.

"We haven't been able to trace the woman, nor the other two. I sent one of our men—a reliable guy, won't have given anything away—to do the rounds of Antibes harbor last night, but he didn't come up with a whisper of any kind. Same with the local police. But I must say, in the woman's place, I wouldn't be hanging around in these parts if I'd read the papers."

Coster nodded. The superintendent might well be right, but Dominique's exact location was only a part of the problem and not necessarily the most important one. He was less concerned with where she actually was than with where the network *thought* she was. He fished out a cigarette, stuck it in his mouth, and toyed with a box of matches, as he stared absentmindedly at the superintendent's mustache.

"Intuition," he muttered. "That's what's needed for this kind of job. Either that or damn good guesswork."

The superintendent was reflecting that you could never go by faces. Take the one opposite

him, for instance. You might easily think that its
owner had just been brought up from the cells. Of
course, the fact that he hadn't shaved had something to do with it. All the same ...

He pulled himself together, cleared his throat
and echoed, "This kind of job?"

Coster gave a start as though he had forgotten
that he was not alone in the room. "Call it war if
you like." He smiled, disassociating himself from
the expression.

Out of his depth, the superintendent returned to
safer ground. "Think she's got a friend in Antibes
who's hiding her?"

"Dunno. I doubt it."

"She could have tucked herself away in one of
the boats."

"Yup. But I doubt that, too. I wouldn't have said
it was her style. Still, it's always possible."

"If she has, we'll soon hear of it. We've got our
informers in Antibes, the same as everywhere else
along the coast."

"Yes, of course ..." Coster got up and held out
his hand. "I expect you're right, though. The odds
are that she's cleared out."

Gratified, the superintendent shook his hand
warmly. But once his visitor had gone, he began to
wonder whether he had not been leading him on
all through their conversation. That was the trouble with the Special Services men—you never
knew what they were really thinking ...

Dominique had awakened several times during the night. The last time, a conviction that the *Vega* was out at sea had sent her rushing to the porthole. But it was only that a warm, humid wind had sprung up, whipping the bay into a miniature storm. As Jean had predicted, the weather had undergone a sudden change.

The sky was overcast, and rain was pattering down on the deck. The *Vega* had developed a heavy roll. Down in the cabin the gusts of wind sweeping through her rigging produced the deep notes of a faraway organ. Dominique could hear Jean moving about in the adjoining deckhouse, accompanied by a clink of metal.

She got dressed and opened the door. The clinking had come from aluminum plates and mugs, which he had laid out on a small folding table, together with an old enameled coffeepot and a plate of bread and jam.

He looked up cheerfully as she came in. "Sleep all right in spite of the filthy weather?"

His mattress was rolled up in a corner, and he had lit an oil stove. Dominique gave a deliberate shiver.

"Cold?"

"I think I've caught one. Either that or flu . . ." She mumbled it without much conviction, conscious that she had always been a bad liar. He merely grunted and glanced at the rain-spattered windows. She sat down at the table.

157

"The coffee smells good."

"Hope it tastes good. Try a cup, anyway. Then if you've nothing better to do, I suggest you go back to bed." Between mouthfuls of the thick slices of bread Jean went on. "As soon as I've finished this, I'll go ashore and rustle up some aspirin. Then I'll concoct Doctor Jean's world-renowned cure-all— hot red wine, cinnamon, and cloves. Guaranteed to do you a world of good. And we'll move the stove into the cabin. You can have some music, too, if you want it. There's a transistor in one of the cupboards. I never listen to it, myself, but it works all right."

"Can't we fix up one of the other cabins? Then you can have yours back."

He stroked his beard and smiled as he had done the evening before. "If you feel up to it . . ."

"I can try."

"Sure. Come and take a look."

He went down three steps to the left of the chart table and opened a door. Following close behind him, Dominique gasped and came to an abrupt halt. However dilapidated they might be, she had expected to see the usual passengers' quarters in a ship of this size; a number of cabins opening out of a long passageway, with a saloon at one end of it. But the *Vega*'s interior had been completely gutted. Nothing was left. Stripped of cabins, passageways, bulkheads, and floors, it was just a huge, empty shell. Daylight, filtering in through the deck skylights and a forward hatchway, revealed a pool of black water splashing about in the hold, some twenty feet below. A vertical ladder led down to it, and level with the door, narrow planks ran across the void from side to side and stem to stern in a rough form of scaffolding.

Jean walked out along one of the planks, and she edged her way gingerly after him.

"Better stay where you are," he called back over his shoulder.

"I'm all right. I've got a head for heights."

She was secretly surprised, all the same, to find how easily she could keep her balance in spite of the pronounced roll. Jumping across to another plank, she held on to one of the masts, which passed through the deck to its base in the hold. Jean had turned to face her, propped up against the other mast, rolling a cigarette.

"Doesn't it make you long to go to sea, living aboard here?" she shouted to him.

He shrugged. "I do some sailing during the season. There's nothing going on in winter, of course. I just pick up odd jobs about the harbor when there are any." Their voices reverberated as though they were in a cave.

She wondered for the first time what his background could be. There was something about him, besides the way he spoke, which scarcely seemed to tally with caretaking and doing odd jobs; it was much easier to envisage him at the wheel of his own yacht. But she was only mildly interested, too mildly to bother to indulge in speculations. It was depressing in the empty hulk, and she was glad when he threw away his cigarette and they returned to the deckhouse.

"Well, that puts an end to those fancy ideas of yours about all the other cabins!" he said, grinning. "As you can see, this is the only habitable part of the ship. There's a small kitchen down below, so it's not too bad." He looked away before adding casually, "If you think you can stand it, you're welcome to stay as long as you like. You won't be putting me out—in fact, you'll be doing me a favor. I'm beginning to talk to myself. Always a bad sign."

"Haven't you any friends?" she asked, surprised.

"Not really. Not since Sando died." He took yellow, paint-stained oilskins off a peg and slipped them on. "I'll go and do the shopping. Bed for you! By the way, any objection to telling me your name?"

There was something she must say to him before he left, and it was a moment before his question penetrated. When it did, she gave him her second name, Danièle. She was still searching for the right words when he reached the door, and to gain a little more time, she blurted out, "Wait a minute! I'll give you some money."

He turned around frowning, "That wasn't the idea."

"I know it wasn't, but if we don't share expenses, I won't stay."

His frown lifted. "Okay, have it your own way. But you don't have to. I'm not broke."

He took the note she held out to him but remained where he was, staring down at her. Finally, he asked, "Something worrying you?"

She avoided his eyes. "It's just that when I got here . . . to Antibes, I mean . . . I was with someone . . . And we had a row . . ."

He put his hands over his ears. "I don't want to hear! It's none of my business. You're landed up here now, and that's all that matters, as far as I'm concerned."

"But it isn't! You must listen!" She was close to tears.

He lowered his hands. "All right, fire away!"

"He was awful to me! I never want to see him again! But he'll be looking for me all over the place. He may come down here, to the harbor. And if he finds me . . ."

"I get it."

"So you mustn't let anyone know I'm here! No one!"

He leaned back against the door. "Just to set your mind at rest, my conversations ashore seldom get beyond 'Good morning' and 'Good evening.' Apart from that, now that I've got someone to keep me company for a while, I'm not crazy enough to start shouting it around. I don't want the wolf pack descending on us, trying to steal you from me. So, push off to bed and relax!"

She smiled at him gratefully. Left on her own, she wondered whether he had believed her. To her own ears, the story had sounded singularly unconvincing. Then, remembering the hint of sadness, or perhaps compassion, in his expression as he had listened to her, she decided that it did not matter whether he had believed her or not, did not matter either to him or to her.

TWELVE

Moscow's instructions to Pierre were to complete the "security operation" forthwith and to find his own replacement for the missing torpedo. Normally, the KGB would have insisted on his tracing the source of the leak that had enabled an outsider to discover the location of one of the network's hideouts; but on this occasion, by a sort of tacit agreement, they left the initiative to the man on the spot and did not refer to it. The growing efficiency of the French counterespionage services made France so dangerous a territory in which to operate that Moscow was driven to concentrate on matters of immediate urgency.

The "regular" Soviet espionage services in France were confining their activities more and more to exercising what influence they could in political and diplomatic circles and picking up items of information by word of mouth. The operational networks, on the other hand, were being exploited to their maximum, and the policy was to retain them in their various sectors for as long as possible. There was no way of knowing what information the Krestowicz woman possessed in addition to the location of the hideout, but she would certainly divulge it in the end to Special Services if they got to her first; consequently she represented a potential, even if not actual, threat to the continued existence of Pierre's network, which had had a remarkable run of success to its credit. It was therefore not surprising that the KGB were more interested in her immediate elimination than in any help she might provide in tracing the leak.

Moscow's message concluded by ordering Pierre to put up at the Hôtel du Bivouac at Cannes and wait there till contacted by the South of France network, which had its headquarters in Marseille. From then on he was to work in close liaison with them. He promptly decided to take over the second torpedo's role himself. He was even more anxious than his masters, in their comfortable offices two thousand miles away, to see the operation suc-

cessfully concluded; and this provoked an urgent
desire to take part in the action personally.

He and Tancred caught the evening train, traveling in different compartments. Tancred left it at
Nice, having arranged for his equipment to follow
by channels known solely to himself.

The Hôtel du Bivouac turned out to be a mod-
est, well-kept establishment opposite the post office. As soon as he got up to his room, Pierre
shaved and had a bath. For the first time in years,
he was released from being just a planner, devis-
ing operations for other men to carry out, with all
the anxieties and occasional regrets that this en-
tailed, and he felt immensely fit and self-confi-
dent. If a trap had been laid in Antibes, he was
convinced that he would succeed in evading it.
But the trap was of secondary importance. All that
really mattered was that the woman should be
there. And despite his innate skepticism, he knew
that she would be, that his reasoning had been
right. It was perhaps less reasoning than a hunter's
intuition . . .

At 10:30, a call came through from Marseille
giving him a name and number to call at 11:00. He
telephoned from a booth in the post office. The
voice at the other end issued brief directions for
finding a "dead-letter box," situated above Le Suquet, opposite the church; in the future, a call to
the hotel would denote that a message had been
left for him in the box. Meanwhile, Antibes and its

vicinity were being systematically scoured by every man the resident network could call on.

Pierre hired a car, lunched on sandwiches, and was on his way to Antibes by 12:30. Heavy rain beat against the Dauphine's windshield as he wound around the coast road, which he had chosen in order to get a first panoramic view of the town from the headland. Tancred, acting independently, would meet him outside the post office at Juan-les-Pins at 6:30. He was confirmed in his first impression that the young man would prove a considerable asset, and his temporary attachment to the network gave the same boost to his morale as the arrival of reinforcements to a commander in the field.

At Nice, Tancred had reserved a room in a small hotel in the Rue Notre-Dame, patronized mainly by elderly tourists and clergymen. He, too, had started off by shaving, in a bedroom made hideous by yellow wallpaper sprinkled with large purple flowers. Now he was stretched out on the bed, closely studying the photograph of Dominique that Pierre had given him at their meeting the evening before.

It had been taken with a telephoto lens, without her knowledge, and blown up. The photographer had done an excellent job, catching her full-face as she came out of an apartment building, her chest thrust slightly forward in what was obviously a characteristic pose. She was wearing a pants suit, and from what could be seen of it, her hair appeared to be coiled up on the back of her neck. Though, according to Pierre, it dated back nearly three years, she would scarcely have changed much in the meantime.

Tancred had seldom been called on to exercise his professional skill on women, particularly one as young as this. The last occasion had been in Amsterdam. A Puerto Rican. But he had not had to search for her, since she had not bothered to hide. Or, to be more exact, she had believed herself so well hidden that . . .

He stroked the photograph gently with his thumb, trying, without any desire to titillate his senses, to picture her body naked—the muscles, the bone structure, and the nervous system. He had a considerable knowledge of anatomy, acquired from a series of lectures during his training course. In addition to anatomy, they had included physiognomy and psychology. Thus, from his last inspection of her face, he had diagnosed a shy, emotional character, a slight tendency toward hyperthyroidism, and a lack of practical ability coupled with a highly developed aesthetic sense. If she was really hiding in Antibes, she would certainly make mistakes. In Antibes or anywhere else, for that matter. She was not the type to hold out long under stress. She was a wild creature—a hare or an antelope, but without their instinct for self-preservation. The nervousness that might well drive her underground would inevitably lead her to reappear at the wrong moment. It was only a question of time . . .

He sat up and painstakingly drew her profile on a sheet of paper, then made several sketches of her face, with the hair long and short, done in various styles. By the time he had registered each one on his mind, visualizing the hair dyed different shades, he was confident that he would recognize her, no matter what changes she had tried to effect in her appearance.

Lying back again, he resumed his study of the photograph. From what he saw in it, he was certain that she had committed the murder without premeditation. If it had been premeditated, she would have lacked the resolution to carry it out when it came to the point. She was one of those women only capable of killing spontaneously, almost accidentally. And she would have run away afterward in panic, haphazardly, which had reacted to her advantage. Had her flight been planned with some kind of logic behind it, the police would have found it far easier to pick up her trail. It could only have been a piece of bad luck that had caused her to be sighted in Antibes.

He turned to the morning paper and one he had kept from the evening before. Once again, he was struck by the curious lack of detail. The earlier paper merely reported that she had been seen, without saying by whom or in what circumstances. The later one only carried a paragraph, stating that inquiries were being pursued. It was obvious that the police were censoring the news, keeping most of it to themselves. Either the police or Special Services.

Nevertheless, from what he had gleaned of the whole business from Pierre, he thought it unlikely that the woman was being used to bait a trap. If the other side suspected her of possessing information of value, their primary concern would be to pick her up as soon as possible. It all amounted to a race to reach her first.

He dressed, had lunch in a pizzeria and caught a bus to Antibes. He was in a genial mood. Admittedly, the weather was disappointing, but the south of France appealed to him, and his mission promised to be more interesting than he had anticipated. In the train on the way down, he had studied a large-scale road map of France and then one of the coast and had come to the conclusion that Antibes's geographical position made it an unlikely place for anyone to pass through in the course of a long journey somewhere else. It was a place to go to with some definite object in view or a place to hole up in when the sea prevented one from going farther.

He was reminded of the small fishing village in Venezuela where he had finally run his target to ground the year before by making roughly the same deduction. The man had been looking for a job, using false Mexican papers and believing like all the others that he was forgotten and safely under cover, blinding himself, like all the others, to the fact that they were *always* found in the end. It was only a question of time and resourcefulness.

He got off at the Antibes bus station and took a short stroll through the old town before making his way to the harbor and concentrating on his business. If you reached a harbor when you were being hunted, you tried to get away by boat. To book a passage openly, you required papers; otherwise, you had to stow away. Whichever you did, you stood a fair chance of success provided you managed to cover your tracks. But once you had been spotted in the neighborhood, you were bound to be picked up while you were making your arrangements. Consequently, something quite unexpected must have happened for the Krestowicz woman still to be at liberty when a widespread search was being made for her throughout the country and she had already been sighted at Antibes. Some extraordinary stroke of luck.

The harbor looked dead and deserted in the rain. It was sheltering nothing but pleasure boats, apart from one small cargo vessel at the end of the jetty, apparently taking on fuel. Hardly the sort of harbor from which to make a successful escape. You could, of course, put to sea in one of the yachts without papers, if you happened to know one of the owners or carried a large sum of money on you. And had the nerve to risk it. But, he decided, it was not an idea that was likely to have occurred to her. All the yachts looked as if they had been laid up for the winter, and at this time of year, it would be virtually impossible for one of them to put out without being noticed.

He walked slowly up and down the quays, but not for long; in the prevailing weather this was liable to attract attention. Retracing his steps, he climbed up onto the ramparts where he could get a comprehensive view of the whole harbor. Below him were hundreds of boats, large and small, sailing yachts and motor launches, one ancient fishing smack pulled up onto the concrete. They seemed to be asleep and uninhabited, but from time to time, a hatchway lifted, and an oil-skinned figure appeared on deck.

It might be difficult to sail away in a yacht, but it would be comparatively easy to hide in one, particularly for a woman who was young and pretty. That constituted a form of international currency, valid anywhere. Yachtsmen were pretty much the same wherever you came across them, susceptible to this kind of currency and always eager to pick it up.

At 6:00, Tancred caught a bus to Juan-les-Pins, where he joined Pierre as arranged outside the post office. In the Dauphine, heading back to Nice, he gave him the benefit of the conclusions to which he had arrived in Antibes.

Pierre listened, smoking one of his small cigars, then said casually, "Yes, I noticed you in the harbor. I was up on the ramparts, more or less where you stood when you left the quay."

Tancred gave him a quick, sidelong glance, impressed that Pierre had seen him when he had failed to see Pierre. It strengthened a growing suspicion that there might be rather more in the old boy than he had imagined at their first meeting.

He said, "So you thought she might be tucked away in the harbor, too?"

"Yes. For slightly different reasons."

Tancred frowned. "What beats me is why the police haven't searched the boats. If we can deduce the woman's there, so can they."

Pierre looked at him as though he found the remark surprising. A moment passed before he explained, "They'd have searched them right away if they'd been in charge." A faint smile hovered around his mouth. "I don't know whether you've come up against counterespionage services much in your line of business, but I've seen quite a lot of them in one place and another. So I can tell you why they've fallen down on this job. It's too simple for them. Their methods work all right when they're up against networks like ours, professionals, but they're useless when they're up against amateurs. None of the old tricks will help them when they're chasing a wretched woman who's running away with no idea, herself, where she's running to. That's your answer."

Tancred said, a little smugly, "Counterespionage have never stopped me."

"It's hardly likely they would. You work alone or maybe with a couple of colleagues, and you work damn fast. Commando stuff. They don't have time to get on to you."

They lapsed into silence. Pierre was taken up with keeping the car on the road. The rain had stopped, but sudden gusts of wind, buffeting against the side, threatened to throw it into a skid. To make matters worse, it was closing time for stores and factories, and long lines of cars and buses were streaming along in both directions, splashing up mud and half blinding him with their headlights.

Once the traffic had thinned out, he said, "We're being backed up by a local network. I'll get them to concentrate on the harbor. Locating the woman obviously comes first, but there's no reason why they shouldn't keep an eye open at the same time for any sign of Special Services operating in the neighborhood, just in case they've been smarter than I think."

"You make it sound damn easy!"

"Should be in this case. From what I know of them, they'll be operating in strength if they're operating at all, and the harbor doesn't offer much cover."

The palm trees along the Promenade des Anglais, with their leaves blown upward by the wind, resembled huge feather dusters. After dropping Tancred in the Place Massena, Pierre turned around and headed back toward Cannes. Branching off to his right, he drove up to Le Suquet and parked the Dauphine behind the church. The terrace opposite was deserted. He crossed the road, sat down on the second bench from the left, and stuck the message, which he had scribbled in Juan-les-Pins, underneath with a piece of chewing-gum. Marseille made a collection daily. Though they could contact him by telephone, the arrangement was not reciprocal. As the resident network, they were entitled to make their own rules.

In Paris the whole of Coster's team had just received orders to proceed to the coast forthwith, traveling independently and taking their equipment with them. Each man was allotted a destination—Golfe-Juan, Cagnes, and elsewhere—within easy reach of Antibes. The team was to be on continual standby day and night, keeping in touch by walkie-talkie, and, immediately on arrival, was to devise a scheme for dividing a semicircle, with Antibes as its center, into sectors, so that a coordinated search could be made should the necessity arise. The said scheme was to be worked out from maps and not by personal reconnaissance.

In the event of an alert, assembly points and map references would be issued by radio, call sign appended.

Coster himself, in a torn pullover and an old American army raincoat, picked up in a second-hand store, was starting on his second liter of red wine in the port of Antibes's least prepossessing bistro. He was not alone at his table, having acquired a couple of new friends: a short, tubby man, with feet that smelled abominably, who claimed to be the captain of an English yacht, and a bleached blond floozie, whom he claimed to be his wife.

All three were speaking English, Coster with a remarkably plausible Liverpool accent. He was telling his companions that he had just come from there after he had lost his ship through no fault of his own, and a rascally insurance company had refused to pay his claim. His presence in Antibes was due to an advertisement he had read in an English paper; some character wanting a captain, but unable, as it turned out, to recognize a man with outstanding qualifications when he saw one. He could have saved his breath and his powers of invention. The other two, as fuddled as he appeared to be, were scarcely listening.

It was the sort of bistro that swarmed with self-promoted captains, wearing caps to prove it. Most of them spent their time, in the thick atmosphere curiously redolent of damp dogs, playing belote and swigging red wine. Three sad-faced Spaniards were standing by the counter, while a fourth, alone in a corner of the room, was alternately taking gulps of marc straight from the bottle and addressing an unheeding audience.

"I don't say you won't find a job here," the tubby man observed to Coster. "What I'm saying is that it won't be as a captain. Not in the winter, it won't. I mean, stands to reason. Now, doing a bit of caretaking on one of the yachts till the season comes around again, that's another matter. D'that suit you?"

"Might do to start off with," Coster mumbled. Bleary-eyed from the smoke and maudlin because it amused him to be, he began a rambling description of the wife and son left behind in England. "Can't let 'em starve, can I? Got to have a sense of responsibility. Wish you could have seen the kid. Bright as a button. Only seven, mind you, and he's this height already . . ." He stretched out his hand as high as he dared. The floozie hiccuped and nodded sympathetically. Coster felt slightly ashamed.

The Spaniard in the corner was beating a tattoo on his chest with his forefinger. "I . . . I know what dying's like . . ." He rocked his chair to and fro perilously on two legs, drew the back of his hand

across his lips and added, dreamily, in stentorian
tones, "It's like when you've had a drop too much.
One moment, you're there . . . and then . . . pffft!"
He raised the forefinger unsteadily in front of his
nose to secure attention for his final, reassuring
message: "That's all it is. Nothing worse than
that . . ."

Come to think of it, he could be right, Coster reflected, vaguely aware that the tubby man had
embarked on a long-winded account of the various
jobs that enterprising friends of his had picked up
around the harbor in winter. He was more concerned, himself, with the responsibility he had assumed in sending for his team and immobilizing
them, probably for several days, in this remote
corner of the country. With nothing to show for it
in the end, as likely as not.

"In the course of an operation not requiring
such extreme measures . . ." He could already see
the adverse report being slipped into his personal
file.

THIRTEEN

"If you get an east wind at this time of year, it can go on for days," Jean remarked.

Dominique was lying on her bed, fully dressed, with a blanket thrown over her legs. She had lost track of the day of the week and the date. All she knew was that the coming night would be the fourth she had spent aboard the schooner. This was as close a relationship as she wanted with the passage of time.

Jean was seated on a folding stool facing the side of the bunk. They were playing an unenthusiastic game of checkers, which he interrupted from time to time with comments on the weather or interpretations of the noises coming from various parts of the ship: "That'll be a halyard slapping against the mast . . . That's from down below, creaking pulley block . . ."

They were living in virtual isolation. Jean scarcely went ashore anymore, having laid in a stock of canned food and cigarettes, as though provisioning for a voyage. He spent a large part of the day on deck, keeping an anxious eye on the moorings in case they started to drag in the storm. "If we aren't careful, we'll wake up one of these mornings and find we've been blown out to sea." In between the times on deck he dozed, smoked, puttered around the deckhouse, brought Dominique endless cups of tea, and reminisced about past voyages.

The cabin had undergone a considerable change. Though Jean had wanted to clean it up when its condition had suddenly dawned on him, Dominique had ousted him and done the necessary scrubbing and polishing herself. She remained below the whole time, not venturing on deck even at night. While turning out the lockers, she had unexpectedly come across old editions of *Madame Bovary* and *Le Rouge et le Noir*, which she reread with nostalgic pleasure, and she had started drawing again, making sketches of Jean, the cabin, and the exterior of the *Vega* as she remembered it, on odd pieces of paper and the backs of charts. Jean showed a flattering interest in her talent, tacking each sketch up on the bulwarks with almost childish pleasure, as soon as one was finished.

The ship had become her entire world, completely detached from the one outside, free from links with what had gone before, and she wanted nothing more. Jean, too, seemed satisfied. Glad of her company, he kept an eye on her with fraternal benevolence, refrained from asking questions, and never made the slightest demands. Every night, he retired early to the deckhouse where his mattress was now permanently installed, and she no longer gave a thought to the bolt on her door.

At 9:00 in the morning of the same day, January 26, Pierre had received a telephone call from Marseille. Twenty minutes later, he was up at Le Suquet to collect the message from the dead-letter box. He read it in his car. "Subject of search is aboard schooner *Vega*, lying in outer harbor, Antibes. Search concluded."

There was no intimation of how the woman had been found and identified, but this was only to be expected: networks always kept their particular methods a closely guarded secret. There was no mention, either, of the size of the schooner's crew. "Search concluded" plainly meant that they now regarded the ball as being in his court. But they would certainly have issued a warning if they had come across any indication of counterespionage activities in or around Antibes. However, this did not guarantee that none existed in view of the short time it had taken them to locate their quarry.

Back at the post office, Pierre telephoned Tancred and arranged a rendezvous in Juan-les-Pins. When they met, he passed on the information received from Marseille, and Tancred took over the Dauphine to drive to Antibes. He did not stay there long: a brief reconnaissance was sufficient for him to decide on a night attack, making his approach from the jetty in a dinghy. He outlined his plan to Pierre in the car, with the aid of a roughly sketched map showing the *Vega's* position, as soon as he got back to Juan-les-Pins.

Pierre pored over the sketch for some time, then shook his head. "Too dangerous. If anyone else is watching the boat, you'll be spotted at once. And if they've laid a trap, you'll be doing just what they're counting on. You'll walk straight into it."

This final phase of the operation was Tancred's sole responsibility, and he was no fonder than Pierre of having his plans questioned. But he asked mildly, "Then what do you suggest?"

"Approach by sea from outside the harbor, using an inflatable dinghy."

"What about the weather? It's damned rough out there!"

"That's precisely why it'd never occur to them that you'd try it."

181

"If *they* exist!" Tancred said sourly.

"That's irrelevant. We've got to operate as though we were certain they are somewhere about. It's a normal precaution. What you'll have to do is hire a car. A large one. Station wagon if you can find it. Then buy a Zodiac—the smallest model, with an outboard motor and oars."

"Outboards make a noise," Tancred objected. "Someone's liable to hear it even if I approach from the sea."

"I've thought of that. While you're getting hold of the stuff in Nice, I'll do a recon of the coast east of Cap d'Antibes. According to the map, there are quite a number of small beaches around here. If we start from one of them . . ."

Tancred interrupted, with raised eyebrows. "*We?*"

"Yes. I'll be going with you." Pierre unfolded a map and spread it across their knees, describing a semicircle between Cap d'Antibes and the harbor entrance with his thick forefinger. "It's quite a short trip, as you can see. We'll use the outboard as far as there, then we'll row. It won't be as tough as you think because with the wind where it is, we'll be swept toward the harbor. When we get about here, we'll stop, and you'll swim the rest of the way. I'll be standing by to pick you up when you come back. You'll need a scuba diver's suit, oxygen bottles, and flippers." He folded the map again before asking, "What's the ship look like?"

"Very old. Practically a wreck."

"Then I'd be surprised if there's more than one man aboard her with the woman, particularly at this time of year. No one's going to pay a crew to do nothing on an old derelict." Pierre took out a thick wad of notes and counted them carefully before handing them over to Tancred. "Buy what we need in Nice, not everything at the same shop. There are plenty of them around the harbor. How about your own stuff?"

"It's arrived."

Pierre cleared his throat and stared at the wall of the casino, facing the parked car. This part of the briefing always made him uncomfortable. He fell back on stilted formality. "I presume Moscow informed you of the special instructions governing operations on French territory?"

Tancred uncrossed his legs and stretched. "Yes. I've got my sleeping pill." He produced a capsule from his breast pocket similar to the one Pierre had given Fedor a few days before and tossed it up in his palm with an almost identical gesture. Then he asked, tranquilly, "You got one, too?"

Pierre nodded. "That woman's cost the network three agents already. Till she's eliminated, we're all in danger."

"I suppose so . . ." Tancred said without interest. "To me, it's just another job."

"Meet me here at two tomorrow morning in the station wagon with all the equipment. You'd better pay your hotel bill before you leave. And see you get some sleep."

Tancred grinned and patted his breast pocket. "If I suffer from insomnia, I can always use this."

By 2:20, the station wagon, driven by Tancred, was rounding the headland on the coast road. Pierre, seated beside him, had left the Dauphine in Juan-les-Pins. Wearing a thick fisherman's jersey and black oilskins, he was chewing on the butt of a dead cigar and looking for the landmarks he had noted earlier in the day.

There were no other cars about as they skirted the sea on their right and the dim outlines of shuttered villas, set back from large gardens, on their left. The whole of the cape presented much the same picture; empty streets and avenues and houses shut up for the winter. The only sign of life came from the lighthouse on the hill, flashing its beam seaward through the fine drizzle.

Tancred slowed down as Pierre touched his arm and pointed to a small cove tucked away in the rocks, then swung the station wagon off the road and glided to a halt in the middle of a cluster of pine trees. It took them half an hour to inflate the dinghy and attach the outboard motor and for Tancred to slip on his rubber scuba diver's suit over a sweater and thick woolen pants. He had cut down his personal equipment to the bare minimum. In a holster hooked to his side, he carried a compressed-air pistol, firing a nine-inch finned harpoon, with an effective range of twenty-five yards. Its silence and the minute device, as deadly and reliable as the poison fang of a snake, fitted in its point made it an ideal weapon for attack at close quarters. Death was virtually instantaneous even from a superficial wound. A second harpoon in a small leather tube was strapped to his left thigh and a sheathed, short-bladed knife to his right. A plastic pouch on his chest contained a flashlight and the capsule, to which he attached little importance.

Calm and concentrated as usual, he checked each item in turn with the slight fussiness of a ski-jumper testing buckles and straps before starting on his run. His complete confidence in his own skills left no room for doubt about the ultimate success of his mission. If he had a worry at all, it was occasioned by his forthcoming trip in the dinghy. An attack of seasickness would mean a minute or two wasted in recovering when he reached his objective. But this was a mere matter of professional pride.

Once they had launched the dinghy and clambered aboard, he was relieved to find that the sea had gone down appreciably since morning. Pierre had unshipped the oars and was rowing with surprising strength and dexterity. It occurred to Tancred again that he had underrated him at their first meeting.

The Zodiac rode the waves well, sliding down into the troughs and bobbing resiliently up again. Over to their left, they could see the lights of Antibes and, opposite, some two miles ahead, the flickering lamps on the jetty. As soon as he judged that they were far enough offshore, Pierre started the motor, and the dinghy's nose began slapping down on the water, raising small columns of spray. The cold was no longer intense, and the wind came in gentle gusts. All in all, it was an ideal night for the job at hand. The overcast sky blacked out the moon, but the lights on shore remained visible enough to give them their bearings.

Farther out the troughs became deeper, and Pierre throttled down to a speed just sufficient to keep the dinghy headed in to the waves. They moved slowly forward in a series of leaps and bounds. As they drew near, he cut the motor altogether and went back to the oars. His prediction had been correct: the sea, sweeping toward the harbor, made his task much easier. He had given the ramparts a wide berth and was now steering a diagonal course beyond a narrow spit of land which finally brought the schooner into view.

When they were within three hundred yards of her, he shipped the oars, leaned forward, and tapped Tancred on the shoulder. Tancred slipped into the water without looking around. He was unaffected by seasickness, but the icy water seeped into his suit, taking his breath away. He floun-

dered about helplessly for a minute or two before
the water warmed up to his body temperature and
he felt fit enough to proceed.

Using an easy crawl, he let the waves carry him
forward, swam underwater for short distances,
and surfaced again, secure in the knowledge that
his approach was silent and invisible. After slowly
circling the *Vega*, he clung to the side of the
dinghy attached to her stern and hung his mask,
oxygen bottles, and flippers over a cleat. Then he
caught hold of a rope dangling from the schooner's
gang-port and climbed aboard.

It was just light enough on deck for him to be
able to dispense with his flashlight. Pierre had rec-
ommended that he start with a quick recon, seeing
as much of the layout as he could through skylights and hatchways. "The cabins in these large
boats are always directly under the skylights, both
sides of the deck . . . But the easiest means of approach will be through the deckhouse. Only, be
careful not to trip over anything lying about on
the deck . . ."

With the door to the deckhouse conveniently
straight in front of him, Tancred saw no point in
the recon. He drew his pistol out of its holster and
pressed down gently on the door latch. After that,
it all happened very quickly. As he opened the
door and bent down to pass through it, a shape
reared up a few feet away from him. In the semi-
darkness it looked enormous. He fired, and it

187

slumped to the floor. The legs gave two or three violent jerks, then there was no further movement.

Tancred switched on his flashlight. He saw a tall, thickset, bearded man, naked to the waist, stretched crookedly across a mattress. The harpoon had struck him full in the chest.

FOURTEEN

Coster had taken up a position on the other side of the bay, opposite the jetty. From where he stood, between two cement breakwaters, he had a clear view of the jetty and the stretch of water leading up to the schooner. But as Pierre had foreseen, he had not thought of an approach being made from the sea.

The *Vega*'s port side was toward him, so that in any case it was impossible for him to see Tancred climbing up from starboard and entering the deckhouse. In actual fact, Coster had lost all hope of anything coming of his planning. He had played the game according to the recognized rules if, like chess, it could be said to have rules; but there was an additional gambit to be reckoned with. The opponent could always refuse to play.

One section of his team was patrolling in the vicinity. The remainder were standing by, ready to reinforce them within a matter of ten minutes. Tonight's full-scale operation, he decided, would be the last. Tomorrow they would stop using the woman as bait and abandon the trap.

Tancred loaded the second harpoon into his pistol and started down the staircase he saw immediately on his left. The ship's roll was heavier than he had allowed for, and he almost lost his balance. He was grateful for the stroke of luck that had enabled him to dispose of the man so quickly. There should be no problem now in eliminating the woman.

Dominique had been awakened by the noise of Jean's fall. She thought she heard him going down the staircase that led to the kitchen, but he was stumbling against the sides, which was quite unlike him. Wondering whether he had been taken ill, she got up and opened the cabin door.

Tancred had not shut the outer door of the deckhouse behind him, and it was swinging gently to and fro. As her eyes accustomed themselves to the darkness, Dominique became aware of Jean's body lying on its back across the mattress. Simultaneously, a narrow beam of light, coming from the staircase, rested for a moment on the opposite wall and then went out.

She just had time to notice the shaft of the harpoon protruding from a dark stain in the center of Jean's chest before there was a soft sound of footsteps mounting the stairs. She rushed out of the deckhouse as Tancred leaped up behind her. Racing down the deck toward the bows in her bare feet, she tripped over a cleat and went sprawling forward. As she scrambled up again, she heard something whistle past just above her head.

Without looking around, she headed for the forward hatchway, desperate to find some kind of cover. Jumping the last few feet, she caught hold of a rung of the vertical ladder with one hand, twisted herself around, and began climbing down into the welcome darkness.

Tancred watched her disappear unconcernedly. He was annoyed with himself for missing her with the harpoon, but it did not matter. In another minute or two he would finish her off with his bare hands. He jumped down the hatchway after her, with his legs drawn up under him, expecting to land in a passageway.

Clinging to the ladder, Dominique felt him brush against her as he hurtled past and, a second later, heard a sharp crack as his body landed on a beam, twenty feet below.

It was only when he saw a woman's outline running along the schooner's deck, followed by that of a man, that Coster realized that he had been outsmarted. They had vanished before he had time to fire and give the woman some protection. Snatching up his walkie-talkie, he barked out orders, then ran toward the motor launch, made fast to one of the breakwaters.

Tancred was conscious but unable to move. He was not in pain, apart from a slight burning sensation running the length of his spine; it was just that his body was completely immobilized, as though it were embedded up to the neck in a block of cement.

After a time, he heard a faint creak and knew that it must have been made by the woman, somewhere up above him in the huge, dark void. He also became aware of the sound of the water, slapping up against his side. Then a third sound caught his attention: that of a motor, far away at first but rapidly getting closer. Pierre must be coming to his assistance.

Dominique was listening to the motor, too. It was now very near. Apart from this and the familiar noises from the schooner, there was nothing else to be heard. Curled up, face downward, on one of the planks, she had no means of knowing whether the man below her in the hold was dead or merely lying low, hoping for her to reveal where she was in order to make another attack on her.

The motor cut out, and there was a bump against the ship's side. Feet moved along the deck, checked, and moved on again, this time more softly. Tancred moistened his lips and tried to cry out. To his relief, his voice emerged at full strength. He called in Russian, "I'm down in the hold, hurt. The woman's somewhere below deck. Hurry!"

A beam from a flashlight shot down from the hatchway, settling on his face, making him blink. He called out again, "Come down, quick! She's somewhere here!"

The light moved upward and began sweeping the planks. Dominique shut her eyes and waited. But nothing happened. Then, at last, a voice shouted in French, "Where the devil are you?" A moment later, the plank on which she was lying vibrated, and a hand gripped her shoulder.

"Hurt?"

When she stood up shakily, Coster told her sharply to stay where she was. Then he went back to the ladder and climbed down to where Tancred lay.

Three hundred yards away, rising and falling with the waves, Pierre had seen the launch put out from the breakwaters and immediately grasped the situation.

He unshipped the oars and began pulling for the open sea.

After ten minutes, he started the motor and headed full speed back to the cove.

A motor launch, manned by three members of Coster's team, came up alongside the *Vega*.

In the depths of the hold, Coster was engaged in interrogating Tancred, watched by Dominique from her perch on the plank. She had not the remotest idea of what was going on. With his flashlight illuminating the Russian's face, Coster patiently asked question after question, despite the total lack of response. "Which part of the coast did you start from?" "How many of you were there?" "Where's the reassembly point?" Interrupted by someone calling his name from up on deck, he shouted back an order to make a thorough search of the stern quarters.

Tancred was trying to gain time after calculating how long it would take Pierre to reach the shore. When he finally decided to speak, it was to ask Coster to get rid of the woman. His body had slipped little by little off the beam, across which it had fallen, and was now lying on a curve of the hull, his head rolling gently from side to side with each movement of the ship. He had begun to be in pain and was breathing through clenched teeth.

Coster turned his flashlight toward Dominique, standing above them as rigid as a sleepwalker, then switched it back to Tancred, and said in Russian, "If we speak Russian, she won't understand."

Tancred gave a grunt. "I don't know Russian. I'm a Finn."

Coster shrugged and asked Dominique to go up on deck. Once she had left, Tancred said little above a whisper, "I'm dying. And there's nothing I can tell you, anyway I was operating on my own. So there's no point in letting me suffer, is there?"

"No point in letting you die, either. You've a chance of pulling through."

Tancred's lips twisted in a wry smile. "You'll let me die if I don't talk. And I won't be allowed to last long if I do. Not much of an outlook."

Coster shook his head. "Not our methods. You'll receive medical attention whether you talk or not. You'll talk in the end, anyway. The point is, if you talk now . . ."

"I know . . . I know . . . You'll give me new identity papers and some ready cash, and let me go. But what's the use? They'll get me sooner or later. They *always* do. If anyone ought to know, I should!" He shut his eyes as a spasm of pain contorted his face. "In the pouch on my chest . . . You took it . . . A capsule . . . Put it in my mouth! . . . You're the only one who knows I'm paralyzed . . . I might have . . ." He opened his eyes again and pleaded like a child, "Please!"

Coster shone his flashlight on the palm of his right hand, where the strychnine capsule lay. He

195

hesitated for a moment, then said gently, "You can't expect to get it for nothing."

"If I tell you . . . the reassembly point?"

"Provided we find someone there, yes. But only if we do."

Tancred's eyelids fluttered. He swallowed his saliva with difficulty before saying, "That doesn't depend on me . . . But if you're satisfied . . . that I told you the right place?"

"Yes, then it's a deal."

Tancred closed his eyes again while he concentrated. If Pierre had decided to land at the cove so as to pick up the station wagon, which would be the rational thing to do, he must be close enough to it by now to make a safe getaway. Consequently, it would do him no harm to divulge this one piece of information. And the dinghy and tire marks would be there to confirm it.

"Cap d'Antibes . . . Just to the east . . . A beach . . . small one . . . with rocks . . . There's a car . . . under the trees."

Pierre was, in fact, heading for the cove because, like Tancred, he realized that it offered him his best chance to escape. A sector around the harbor would inevitably be sealed up, but there was no reason for it to extend to the cape. He had made a wide semicircular detour to avoid any risk of being spotted from shore and, enveloped in
196

darkness, unmolested by searchlights, was beginning to feel safe.

In view of the time lapse between Tancred
climbing aboard the schooner and the launch putting out from the breakwaters, he must have
achieved his mission. The race had been won with
a few minutes to spare, and there was no longer
any danger of the woman talking. Basically this
was all that mattered, though it looked as if success had cost the life of another agent, the fourth,
since he could count on Tancred obeying the special instructions if trapped on board. Count on him
as confidently as he had counted on Fedor.

There was, of course, a possibility that Tancred
had managed to dive overboard without being
seen before the launch came alongside; but even if
this were so, he felt no qualms at having failed to
wait and pick him up. He himself was responsible
for a whole network. Self-preservation was a duty.
Moscow would certainly approve his decision.

Glancing back, he caught sight of a feather of
spray, slicing through the darkness, a long way behind him. At first, he took it for a comber, but it
came on too steadily, maintaining the same outline, to be that. It must be thrown up by the bows
of a launch, presumably sent out to search for the
boat which had brought Tancred within swim-
ming distance of the schooner. But it could not
have spotted him; otherwise he would have found

himself ringed by a searchlight. There was, when he came to think of it, something odd in the fact that they had not switched one on: ordinarily, they should have been using it to sweep the sea ahead of them. They were acting as though they knew exactly where they were going.

By now, he was very close to shore. Even if they were chasing him, he had much too good a start on them to be caught. His judgment had been right in heading back to the cove rather than making for the nearest spit of land. The station wagon would be there, waiting for him, whereas they would have to continue the hunt on foot.

He cut the engine as he came alongside a flat rock, jumped out, and let the dinghy drift away. Instinctively, with his usual precaution, he had drawn his revolver. A wave, creeping up behind him, sent him sprawling onto the pebbles and knocked it out of his hand. He groped around for it for a few seconds before giving up and running to the car. He could just hear the purr of the launch's motor, still a long way offshore.

Backing out through the pine trees, without switching on his lights, he reached the road, then headed down it, but he had covered scarcely a quarter of a mile before a car with blazing headlights emerged from somewhere to his right and swerved to a halt directly in his path. Two figures emerged from it while it was still moving, threw themselves down in the ditch, and fired a burst from submachine guns into his tires.

He automatically stamped on his brakes. The station wagon skidded along the shoulder, slued around, and came to rest with its rear smashed against a tree. In the moment that followed, nothing happened. The two men remained where they were, with their guns leveled at the car, and Pierre sat motionless, gripping the steering wheel. It lasted only a few seconds, but long enough to enable him to take the capsule from the pocket of his oilskins and bite into it. One swift movement of his hand would do it. There was still time . . . Time, too, if he preferred, to jump out and start running and be mowed down by the machine guns.

But he did neither. His mind was on Fedor, picturing him with appalling clarity as he took that simple, final step.

A third man got out of the car ahead. He switched on a flashlight, directing its beam at Pierre's face through the windshield, then walked slowly toward the station wagon, his arms by his side. Pierre bent forward, rested his forehead on the wheel, and closed his eyes. He knew now that he was going to talk. After all these years, it had suddenly come to him, like a revelation, that life— his life, anyway—was beyond price. He could not bring himself to surrender it.

Tancred heard the sound of feet on the ladder, and the beam from a flashlight dazzled him again for a moment before moving on to the area beside him. Coster squatted down and held out his open palm, with the capsule lying on it, as he had done a short while before.

"Back already?" Tancred asked in a whisper. He was puzzled and alarmed. It would have taken them longer than this to check.

Coster slid the capsule between finger and thumb and held it to Tancred's lips without replying.

Tancred frowned and said, "Not yet." Then added, "How . . . ?"

"A launch to drive him back to the cove. A car to intercept him. Very quick and efficient. I split my team in two—one section aboard here with me and the rest waiting on shore. Kept in touch by walkie-talkie."

Tancred stared at him disbelievingly. "You didn't take him . . . alive?"

"Not a scratch on him. No poison. No nothing. Code name: Pierre. And yours, I gather, is Tancred. Russian torpedo. Arrived in this country, via Finland, on the twenty-third to eliminate Dominique Krestowicz."

The veins on Tancred's face stood out. He seemed to be making an agonizing effort to sit up. "He's been talking?"

"Yes, he's been talking," Coster said dryly. He

felt no sense of triumph; merely very tired. "He's blown the whole of his network. Threw in the location of Marseille's dead-letter box at Le Suquet for good measure."

Tancred opened his lips, and Coster slipped the capsule into his mouth. The Russian's jaws moved gently up and down as though he were sucking a piece of candy. Presently, they stopped. His eyes were fixed unblinkingly on some spot in the darkness above Coster's shoulder. Then an expression of utter disgust crossed his face, and he spat the capsule out, noisily, with the last of his remaining strength.

Coster gave a nod of comprehension and stood up. "We've an ambulance standing by on the quay. The doctor's come aboard. I'll send him down to you." As he reached the foot of the ladder, he turned around, and said slowly, "That woman you were supposed to kill. She didn't know anything. A friend of hers happened to follow her husband by pure chance. The rest was jealousy. But networks never take human emotions into consideration, do they? Seems a pity from your point of view. You'd have been saved the trip . . ."

Jean's body had been removed from the deckhouse. His mattress, eiderdown, and blanket still lay in the corner. It was 5:00 in the morning, and the rain had started coming down again in torrents. Dominique was sitting on a stool by the chart table, with her head in her hands. Coster leaned against the bulwark opposite her, his hands deep in the pockets of his oilskins.

He was saying, ". . . So you're in the clear. You stumbled on something without realizing what it was, but after that, your husband and the woman with him couldn't have risked letting you leave that apartment alive, however much he may have wanted to. Sounds melodramatic, but it's true." He looked at her completely deadpan. "Unfortunately for them, you beat them to the draw. Legitimate act of self-defense in the circumstances. There won't even be a trial. The papers will pipe down, too."

She scarcely seemed to take it in. When she spoke, it was to ask, "Have you been watching the boat all this time?"

"For the last few days. It looked to us as if the network was bound to suspect you of knowing more than was good for them. We suspected it, ourselves, for that matter, so . . ."

Dominique turned toward Jean's mattress. Tears were coursing down her cheeks. She brushed them away roughly with her fingertips. "He got killed instead of me. If he hadn't been sleeping there because he'd given me his cabin, I'd never have heard that awful man."

"You're not to blame," Coster said. "The truth is, I slipped up. The idea was to jump them before they ever reached the boat, but I hadn't reckoned on them coming in from outside the harbor. Thank God, you had a stroke of luck and managed to escape all on your own. You've been damned lucky, one way and another, from the beginning."

With her mind still on Jean, Dominique said, "He wasn't!"

"No," Coster agreed, "but he must have known it was liable to happen to him sooner or later. You haven't asked me how you were traced. By us and the others."

"It doesn't much matter now, does it?"

"It might . . . The day after you settled in here, an informer reported it to the police. Then we took steps to leak it to the other side in the hope that they'd fall into our trap. It was easy enough to do. A little careless talk here and there. It was sure to reach them in the end. Plenty of ears to pick it up once the papers had announced that you'd been seen in Antibes. The informer . . ."

Coster paused, conscious that he had Dominique's full attention at last. She had raised her head and was staring at him with a sort of puzzled dismay. He jerked his chin in the direction of the mattress.

"The informer reported that you were aboard his boat just as a matter of routine. He had no idea who you were at the time. There are always a few characters like him, hanging around harbors. Small-time smugglers or ex-convicts. The police let them be in exchange for occasional tip-offs, passing the word when anyone at all suspicious turns up. In this case, we asked a bit more of him, asked him to keep you safely on board and see you didn't go ashore. Very important if our scheme were to work. The Antibes police slipped him a few francs, and he was only too happy to oblige. They've known him for years."

"I just can't believe it!" Dominique broke in. "He was so . . . so . . ."

"Nice?" Coster suggested with gentle irony. "Those guys always are. They wouldn't get anywhere if they weren't." He grinned. "It's only good guys like me who can afford to be bastards . . ."

It was not till the following day that Sylvia's body was fished out of the Rhône, at the Guillotière. It had been in the water for over a week and must have been caught up on the bottom or against a column of the bridge before eventually being swept downriver again.

Despite this, there was no trouble in identifying her. Among all his other disclosures, Pierre had given a full account of Kola's last mission, or, rather, as much as he knew of it from the instructions he had issued, himself. This was the way in which he earned small extensions of his life-span. Installed in the basement of a house with an unlisted telephone number, he filled tape after tape, unflaggingly. Once he had started talking, his appetite for it grew.

When he finally dried up, he would be allowed to go, armed with a new passport and a small sum of money, following the customary practice. But the bullet with his name on it was already waiting in Moscow for the trap to open and the pigeon to flutter out.

Tancred could have told him that he had not a chance in hell of escaping it, but he would not have believed him. They never did ...

FIRST BLOOD
by David Morrell

Nobody in the small Kentucky town knew his name was Rambo; all they knew was that he was a stranger . . . and that he looked like trouble. Rambo was trouble. The army had trained him in the art of killing, and now he did not know how to stop.

P1843   A FAWCETT CREST BOOK $1.25

FAWCETT

Wherever Paperbacks Are Sold

THE CHILLING
NEW BESTSELLER
BY THE AUTHOR OF
PSYCHO

NIGHT-WORLD
by Robert Bloch

NIGHT-WORLD begins when Karen Raymond arrives at a private sanitarium in the San Fernando Valley to visit her husband. She finds the place strewn with bodies. Her husband and four other patients are missing. Karen's race against time—to find the killer, who might be her husband—makes *NIGHT-WORLD* the most terrifying novel since *PSYCHO*.

"An arresting thriller."—*Saturday Review*.

"*NIGHT-WORLD* speeds along at a terrifyingly fast pace."—*Library Journal*

M1845   A FAWCETT CREST BOOK   95¢

FAWCETT

Wherever Paperbacks Are Sold

If your bookdealer is sold out, send cover price plus 15¢ each for postage and handling to Mail Order Department, Fawcett Publications, Inc., Greenwich, Connecticut 06830. Please order by number and title. Catalog available on request.

FAWCETT CREST BESTSELLERS

THE STEPFORD WIVES *Ira Levin*	P1876	$1.25
FREE & FEMALE *Barbara Seaman*	Q1878	$1.50
ENEMIES, A LOVE STORY *Isaac Bashevis Singer*	P1877	$1.25
FIRST BLOOD *David Morrell*	P1843	$1.25
ANIMA *Marie Buchanan*	P1827	$1.25
A FALCON FOR A QUEEN *Catherine Gaskin*	P1828	$1.25
THE GODS THEMSELVES *Isaac Asimov*	P1829	$1.25
CAPTAINS AND THE KINGS *Taylor Caldwell*	X1819	$1.75
OUT OF THE DARK *Norah Lofts*	P1822	$1.25
THE OPTIMIST'S DAUGHTER *Eudora Welty*	P1820	$1.25
MY NAME IS ASHER LEV *Chaim Potok*	Q1807	$1.50
THE GODFATHER PAPERS *Mario Puzo*	P1797	$1.25
THE GODFATHER *Mario Puzo*	A1708	$1.65
POOR COUSINS *Ande Manners*	P1809	$1.25
THE ASSASSINS *Elia Kazan*	A1795	$1.65
MONDAY THE RABBI TOOK OFF *Harry Kemelman*	P1785	$1.25
TALES OF THE SOUTH PACIFIC *James A. Michener*	P1790	$1.25
THE DRIFTERS *James A. Michener*	X1697	$1.75
BEAR ISLAND *Alistair MacLean*	P1766	$1.25
RABBIT REDUX *John Updike*	Q1753	$1.50
A WORLD BEYOND *Ruth Montgomery*	M1755	95¢
THE OTHER *Thomas Tryon*	P1668	$1.25

FAWCETT

Wherever Paperbacks Are Sold

If your bookdealer is sold out, send cover price plus 15¢ each for postage and handling to Mail Order Department, Fawcett Publications, Inc., Greenwich, Connecticut 06830. Please order by number and title. Catalog available on request.